BORED T[C]

Marie hates the sma... lives. She yearns to escape ... Stamfield, and enjoy the excitement of life in the big city. Sometimes she feels this place will kill her if she doesn't get out. So when she goes missing, everyone thinks she's run away to find her dream. But the trail of clues she leaves behind ends much closer to home. Perhaps Marie found excitement in Stamfield after all—excitement beyond her wildest nightmares . . .

P●INT CRiME

BORED TO DEATH

Margaret Bingley

Galaxy

CHIVERS PRESS
BATH

First published 1997
by
Scholastic Children's Books
This Large Print edition published by
Chivers Press
by arrangement with
Scholastic Children's Books
1999

ISBN 0 7540 6071 3

British Library Cataloguing in Publication Data available

Bingley, Margaret, 1947-
    Bored to death. - Large print ed. - (Point Crime)
    1. Detective and mystery stories 2. Young adult fiction
    3. Large type books
    I. Title
    823. 9'14[J]

ISBN 0-7540-6071-3

Printed and bound in Great Britain by
REDWOOD BOOKS, Trowbridge, Wiltshire

CHAPTER ONE

Tess wandered into her sister's bedroom and picked her way carefully through the mass of discarded clothes lying on the floor.

'Are you throwing some of these out?' she asked eagerly, picking up a long flowing Indian-style skirt.

Marie shook her head and her long blonde hair swung from side to side. She looked just like one of the models used to advertise shampoo on the television. Tess tried in vain to repress a flicker of envy. She'd have given anything to have hair like that, instead of the short brown curly mop that she'd inherited from her mother.

'I'm trying to find something to wear!' exclaimed Marie. 'I really need this job. If I have to spend the next ten weeks in Stamfield, with nothing to do and nowhere to go, I shall die of boredom.'

'It's only a waitress they want, not a film star,' Tess pointed out. 'I'd have thought almost anything would do for the interview.' She thought to herself that even if Marie wore an old sack she'd still look wonderful. She had the knack of looking good no matter what she wore. Skirts that made Tess look frumpy and old fashioned were transformed the moment Marie put them on, and her sister couldn't understand why. It was infuriating.

Marie smiled her enigmatic smile, the one that drove the boys wild, and gave Tess a pitying look. 'That's where you're wrong, Tess. Just think of all the girls in this town who'll be chasing after the job. The Skylark Motel aren't going to ask us to show them how well we carry trays or take down orders, so how do you think they're going to choose the successful candidate?'

Tess picked up a low-cut blouse and wondered where Marie had got it from. It was satin and obviously expensive. Normally Marie's clothes, like Tess's and most of their friends', came from the Saturday market. 'Where did you get this?' she asked.

To her surprise, Marie snatched it

away from her. 'Leave that alone! You've got gunk on your fingers and I don't want it marked.'

'Oh, sorry. I was keeping an eye on little Suzie next door while her mother went shopping. It must be some of the plasticine.'

Marie sighed. 'I don't know how you can possibly bear the thought of spending your life looking after small children—they drive me mad. What do you think of this?' she added, pulling on a pastel blue Lycra dress with thin shoulder straps.

'Looks good,' admitted Tess. 'Rather like a long vest, but it suits you!'

For a brief moment Marie giggled, but then she resumed her critical self-examination in the mirror and brushed some more mascara on to her already thick lashes. 'The girl who gets this job will be the one the interviewer remembers,' she said slowly. 'In other words, I have to make an impact.'

'Suppose it's a woman who's doing the interviews? Don't you think the length of the dress might go against you then?' suggested Tess.

'It's a man. Linda told me. She went for the interview yesterday.'

'Then the job's probably yours,' said Tess. She tried to say it casually, without letting jealousy show. After all, at sixteen she was too young to try for the job anyway, and she was quite used to the fact that every male who came into contact with Marie fell under her spell. She was pretty, friendly and good fun—everything a man wanted, and only Tess knew that what they saw wasn't what they'd get if they got to know her properly. Even Tess, who was closer to her than anyone else, wasn't certain that she completely understood her sister. Marie liked to have secrets, and there was a certain point at which she cut other people off.

When she did this to Tess it hurt, although she didn't think Marie realized quite how much. Once, when Tess had tackled her about it, she'd looked startled for a moment. Then she'd smiled one of her dazzling smiles. 'It's not that I don't trust you,' she'd said, giving her sister a rare hug, 'but you know what the parents are like. If I don't tell you things it's because I don't want you having to lie to them. You're not like me, you'd feel bad about it. I'm protecting you, not trying to shut you out. Honestly, Tess, it's true. You're about the only person in the world I really trust, and I tell you everything I can.'

Now, as Marie pulled the dress down over her slender body and posed in front of her sister with one hand on her hip and the other held out to the side, Tess suddenly remembered that conversation.

'How's that for the height of sophistication?' Marie asked.

Tess laughed. 'How about "101 uses for your dad's old vest"?'

'Jealousy will get you nowhere,' retorted Marie. 'What are you up to this afternoon? Seeing Ian?'

Ian was Tess's boyfriend and had just finished taking his A-levels at the sixth form college attended by Marie. If his results were good he was planning on taking a year out to work his way round Europe before taking up a place at university.

'Yes, we're going into town for a couple of hours. I need some new Doc Martens and Pascal's has them in their sale, but only the purple ones.'

'They make you look as though you've got size ten feet,' said Marie. 'Still, if Ian doesn't mind why should I? By the way, have you told Mum and Dad that Alec and I are going to the cinema with you and Ian tonight?'

Tess sat down on the edge of Marie's bed and nodded. 'Yes, but only because I thought you really were! Why are you letting Alec down again? It's horrible having to make up things all the time, and it isn't fair on him either.'

'He's used to me,' said Marie lightly. 'We went out two nights ago, so he isn't exactly neglected. Besides, I make it up to him when I do see him!'

'Sometimes,' said Tess in a low voice, 'you can be really horrible.'

Marie's cornflower-blue eyes opened wide in surprise. 'What have I said?'

'It doesn't matter. I just hope one day you find out that it doesn't always pay to use other people quite so ruthlessly.'

6

Marie frowned. 'Come on, Tess! I don't *use* them—I always ask first, and I never tell them lies. Alec understands me.'

'He fancies you like mad.'

'Well, that's not my fault, is it? Anyway, I like him too.'

'You might not lie,' said Tess with a sigh, 'but you don't always tell the whole truth. And you do lie to Mum and Dad.'

'No, I don't,' laughed Marie, 'you do! How do I look?' She saw that Tess was still frowning. 'Remember, you're in no position to start preaching. Ian doesn't know everything about you, does he? But I do. So, how do I look?'

'Neat,' conceded Tess, but she was shaking with temper and had to force herself to smile. It wasn't fair. She'd only been out twice with Jean-Paul, a visiting French student, before she realized that he wasn't worth jeopardizing her relationship with Ian for. Yet somehow Marie had found out, and whenever Tess tried to interfere in her life she would remind Tess that she had the power to hurt her.

'Wish me luck then,' called Marie, as she ran out of the room and down the stairs.

'You won't need it,' said Tess crossly to herself as she absent-mindedly picked up some of the clothes from the floor where Marie had left them. 'If you want the job badly enough you're bound to get it.' With one final glance at the expensive satin blouse she went back to her own room, which was relatively tidy by comparison.

By the time Tess and Ian got back from town it was nearly five, and after arranging to meet up at the cinema at half-past seven they parted company at Tess's house.

'You say Marie's standing Alec up?' said Ian. Tess nodded. 'Well, he'll probably still want to see the film with us. You won't mind, will you?' asked Ian, as he walked away.

'Of course not,' said Tess, although she did mind a bit because it meant that she and Ian had less time alone together. However, she didn't feel she could say much because Alec was providing yet another alibi for Marie, and anyway he was good company. He was also exceptionally handsome, but Tess didn't think about that too much since in her experience good-looking eighteen-year-old youths went out with beautiful girls like Marie, not reasonably attractive ones like her. Life was easier, Tess had learned, if you didn't spend too much time longing for things that were out of reach. That was part of Marie's trouble and the reason why she sometimes got depressed.

As Tess went indoors Marie came running down the stairs and it was clear from her laughter and bright eyes that she wasn't in a black mood now: quite the reverse, in fact.

'I got it!' she shouted in glee.

'The job?'

'Yes! I can start tomorrow night. Isn't that brilliant?'

Tess stared at her. 'But I thought there were two more days of interviews. Katy Martin goes for one tomorrow.'

'Keith couldn't resist me,' Marie said, with a laugh. 'It must have been the vest!'

'Keith?'

'Keith Palmer—he owns the Skylark Motel.'

Tess frowned. 'What was the owner doing interviewing prospective waitresses?'

Marie shrugged. 'Who cares? I got the job and that's all that matters.'

'What are the hours like?' asked Tess.

Marie shrugged. 'Not bad, but it's shift work, which is a bit of a pain.' She lowered her voice. 'It might make it difficult for me to meet *you know who* so often.'

Just then their mother came in and the conversation stopped. While Marie was recounting her success once more, Tess went up to her room and sat down in front of her dressing-table mirror. She stared at her reflection, but she wasn't thinking about herself at all. She was thinking about Marie.

It had started a few months earlier.

Marie had asked Tess to give her an alibi for an evening while she went out with what she described as 'an incredible new guy'. Tess had done as she'd asked, but when the request was repeated a few days later she'd asked why such an incredible guy had to be a secret.

Marie had muttered a few things about having a right to a private life and not wanting her mother spoiling things, but finally she'd admitted that the man was married. 'He's separated,' she'd assured Tess, 'but you know what a fuss the parents would make. I'll tell them when his divorce comes through.'

Knowing exactly what sort of a fuss they'd make, and the kind of scenes that would follow, Tess had reluctantly agreed, but despite continued efforts she'd still been unable to prise the name of the man out of Marie. 'I'm protecting you again,' her sister had said firmly. 'If you don't know, you can't tell.'

The longer the secret relationship went on, the more deeply involved Tess became in the lies and cover-ups. She was starting to feel really bad about it, but couldn't think of any way out. According to Marie the divorce was due 'any day now', and Tess hoped that was true. It would lift the guilt from her shoulders and also mean that Alec, who deserved better, wouldn't be stood up so often.

Ian didn't see Alec's involvement in quite the same way as Tess did. 'He doesn't have to keep seeing her; he must think she's worth the hassle,' he'd pointed out. 'If you ask me he's off his trolley, but they seem to have a great time when they do go out, and Alec's experienced enough to make up his own mind, so don't waste your sympathy on him.'

Ian was right, Tess knew that, and on the nights when Alec wasn't with her and Ian pretending to be part of a foursome because Marie had stood him up at the last moment, he was always on the town with a different girl. However, she still felt that Marie was treating him badly.

'You're the one she's being unfair on,' Ian had said that afternoon when she'd raised the subject. 'Why don't you tell her you won't cover up for her any more?'

Because I'm scared of losing you, thought Tess, but she couldn't say that.

Now, thinking about it, Tess knew it was also because despite Marie's looks and popularity with the boys, she felt sorry for her. Life in Stamfield drove Marie mad. She hated the small market town set in the peaceful Lincolnshire countryside. Even the new bowling alley, cinema and nightclub, which had been built over the past few years as southerners moved into the area, snapping up the cheaper houses and increasing the population, didn't satisfy her. Marie wanted the bright lights of London, and until she could get enough qualifications to go there and find work in the fashion industry she was stuck in what she thought of as the most boring backwater in the world.

Tess knew that the excitement of this forbidden relationship was something to make Marie's days more interesting, and that she probably thought of it as the kind of thing girls did in big cities. It was as though she was practising for the future and Tess, who loved Stamfield, could still understand the despair of someone who didn't. That was why she'd gone along with it so far.

'Perhaps the job will mean the end of the relationship,' she murmured to her image. 'Maybe once she's busy with the job she'll lose interest in her Mystery Man.'

'Who are you talking to, Tess?' asked her mother and Tess jumped with surprise.

'Myself,' she admitted. 'I'm probably going mad. It's because I haven't got anything to do for the next ten weeks.'

'There's plenty you can do if you want to,' said her mother. 'Your cupboards need . . .' Tess tuned out.

*   *   *

That evening Tess and Marie left home together, having tried to get away before their mother spotted them but failed. Tess's heart sank; she was always afraid that her face would give

14

away the fact that she wasn't telling the truth. Marie was far more skilful at deception than she was.

'What's on at the cinema?' asked their mother.

'That new thriller,' replied Tess, glancing at her watch as though they were already late in the hope this would end the conversation.

'Are you bringing Ian and Alec back after?'

Marie smiled brightly at their mother. 'We might, but Alec starts work at the garage so early in the morning he'll probably go straight home. It's a long film.'

'Come on,' said Tess, tugging at her sister's arm. 'We'll keep them waiting if we don't go now.'

'Enjoy yourselves, and try to persuade Alec to drop in more often—we see plenty of Ian!' called their mother. Tess felt even worse about what they were doing.

'When's this guy's divorce coming through, Marie?' she probed. 'I'm tired of telling lies for your sake.'

Marie's mouth tightened a little and

she lifted her chin defiantly. 'It won't be long. He's trying to hurry it up but his wife's being difficult.'

'Difficult? I thought it was virtually cut and dried!' exclaimed Tess.

'It is, but the money's not settled. I've got to rush, he hates being kept waiting. Don't go home without me, will you? I'll meet up with you and Ian at the Burger King at half ten, OK?'

'I suppose so,' said Tess reluctantly.

Marie gave her one of her most dazzling smiles. 'I won't forget this, Tess. One day I'll do the same for you.'

'I shan't go out with married men,' retorted Tess. 'It can't be worth all these lies, Marie.'

'Believe me, it is!' laughed her sister, and with a quick wave of the hand she vanished round the corner.

Alec and Ian were already outside the cinema talking about the increased amount of repair work the garage was getting. Tess hated it when they talked about cars, and Ian laughed at the expression on her face.

'Change of subject required, Alec. Tess only likes cars to get her from A to B. How they work doesn't interest her.'

Alec raised his eyebrows. 'What will you do when your car breaks down on the motorway then, Tess?'

'Call the AA on my mobile phone,' she retorted. 'Will we get in? This queue's horrendously long.'

Ian checked where they were standing. 'We'll get in. The people standing next to the Co-op window won't though; that's the cinema's limit.'

'What a mine of useful information you are,' remarked Alec, smiling at a pretty auburn-haired girl who was walking by. She smiled back at him.

'Who was that?' asked Tess.

Alec shrugged. 'No idea. I hoped you'd know.'

'If I did I wouldn't tell you—you've broken enough hearts as it is,' retorted Tess.

'Not as many as your sister,' replied Alec.

'No quarrelling,' said Ian quickly. 'Remember, this is a fun foursome tonight!' The queue began to move forward at last. 'You hate covering up

17

for her, don't you?' whispered Ian as they reached the box office.

Tess nodded.

'Then don't!' urged Ian. 'Tell her how you feel and she'll have to come out into the open. If it weren't for you and Alec she wouldn't have got away with it for so long.'

'But she's in love with him,' hissed Tess as they took their seats. 'She'd be shattered if I let her down.'

'If you ask me, the only person your sister's ever been in love with is herself,' said Ian quietly. Tess didn't have the chance to respond because at that moment the lights were dimmed.

When the film was over the three of them made their way to the Burger King where Marie was to join them. They were deep in conversation about what they'd seen when she arrived, but the moment she materialized at their table all discussion ended as Marie worked her magic on both Alec and, Tess was amused to notice, Ian.

'Have a good evening?' asked Alec, his dark blue eyes unfathomable as he studied her.

'Out of this world!' laughed Marie. 'How was the film? Tell me the plot quickly in case the parents ask me something.'

'Read the review,' said Tess, suddenly irritated by the fact that both Ian and Alec were staring in open admiration at her sister's long tanned legs, which were set off by a short canary yellow skirt, while the striped yellow and green halter top emphasized her top half equally well.

'I'd rather Alec told me,' said Marie, sitting down next to him and resting her head close to his. 'Who played the temptress, Alec? I can't remember.'

When Marie was behaving like this Tess always found it hard to stay good tempered, and tonight was no exception. Suddenly she stood up. 'I'm going home,' she announced. 'My head's aching.'

Ian immediately got up and left with her, but Alec and Marie remained behind. 'We'll catch up with you in a few minutes,' called Alec, glancing over his shoulder at them. 'I'll just outline the plot to Marie.'

'Have you really got a headache?' Ian asked when they got outside.

Tess shook her head. 'No, but I hate watching Marie flirt with Alec when she's meant to be in love with this other guy.'

'I know she's older than you, but I think you let her get away with murder,' said Ian, slipping his arm round Tess's shoulders and pulling her close to him. 'She enjoys winding you up, anyone can see that.'

'She doesn't!' protested Tess. 'I don't think she realizes what she's doing. It's as though she's trying to prove something to herself all the time.'

'I'm glad you're not like her,' whispered Ian, kissing Tess gently on the cheek.

'Are you?' Tess pulled away to look carefully at him. 'You seemed quite smitten by Marie a few minutes ago.'

Ian laughed. 'Smitten by her outfit, sure, but not her personality. I like a girl who's attractive and has a nice personality too.'

'Marie's got plenty of personality,' protested Tess.

20

'Can we talk about you, or at least us, for a change?' asked Ian, putting his arms round her. With a sigh of pleasure Tess relaxed against him.

'Come on, you two!' called Marie a few seconds later as she hurried up the road. 'Time we were getting home.'

'Give us a break,' said Ian irritably. 'You've had your fun for the evening—what about the rest of us?'

'You've been going out for over a year,' laughed Marie. 'You get plenty of time together. Besides, I need an early night. I start at the Skylark Motel tomorrow.'

'Would the earth stop turning if you asked it to?' enquired Alec, coming up slowly behind them.

Marie grinned. 'Who knows? Shall I give it a try? Earth, stop turning! No, it's still on the move, never mind. *Tess, come on!*'

Ian and Alec watched the two sisters walking up the road towards their house.

'Stunning, isn't she?' remarked Alec.

'Which one?' asked Ian.

Alec smiled. 'Marie, of course. I

21

know Tess is your girlfriend, and she's a really nice girl, but when you look at Marie . . .' His voice tailed off.

'When I look at Marie these days I see trouble,' retorted Ian, who didn't like the implied criticism of Tess.

'It's the kind of trouble I wouldn't mind being involved in,' laughed Alec.

CHAPTER TWO

The next three weeks of the long summer holiday turned out to be incredibly hot, and Tess and Ian spent a lot of their time at the local swimming pool or simply lazing around near the river that ran through Stamfield and out into the fens.

'How's Marie enjoying her job?' asked Ian one afternoon, as they sat on the river bank watching Ian's mongrel dog Rufus rush around, trying to catch the ducks as they flew on and off the water.

'She loves it,' said Tess. 'I hear more about the job than I do about her unknown boyfriend, which makes a nice change.'

'No chance of any work for me, I suppose? Dad says we need the cash and I don't think he believes me when I say there isn't any casual work around.'

'Marie says the motel's fully staffed, although according to her they could do with more people, but the owner keeps a tight rein on the purse strings.'

'Pity,' muttered Ian. 'Even the supermarkets don't need shelf-stackers this summer.'

Tess nodded. 'Don't I know it! I tried them all before term ended. I think the temporary jobs must go to relatives of people who work there full time. Maybe next year I'll get work at the Skylark. I'll be old enough by then.'

'Wouldn't you mind the shift work?' asked Ian.

'Marie says you get used to it. She's on four to ten tonight. She finds that the worst because it spoils your afternoon and your evening.'

'This time next year I'll be in Europe,' said Ian suddenly. 'What bliss! Imagine it: backpacking around

France, stopping at the odd café for a coffee and a croissant—bliss!'

Tess felt her stomach do a tiny lurch. She'd known for ages that he was planning to go as soon as his A-level results came through but she hadn't really thought about it too much. The realization that they wouldn't be a couple for much longer was horrible, and she wished Ian hadn't mentioned it.

He took hold of her hand and squeezed it gently.

'You knew I was going, Tess. It's only for a year.'

She nodded. 'Sure, no problem. It just sounded sort of odd, you know— thinking about me sitting here by the river on my own next year.'

'You can bring Rufus if you like!' joked Ian, trying to lighten the mood.

'If I'm working I suppose it won't be so bad,' said Tess. 'Sometimes I think Marie's right about this place—it *is* boring.'

'Well, I'm not bored right now,' murmured Ian, moving closer to her. Tess snuggled up against him, but just then they heard the sound of a bicycle bell and a small boy of about ten careered towards them, totally out of control. He fell off and landed at Ian's feet, cutting both his knees badly in the process. By the time Tess had comforted him and wiped him clean they had to leave.

'For a boring underpopulated town we seem to get a lot of interruptions,' complained Ian.

'At least we're on our own tonight,' said Tess. 'Alec isn't coming to the barbecue with us, is he?'

Ian shook his head. 'No, he said he'd got something on. I'll call round for you about eight, OK?'

'Sure. See you then,' called Tess, grateful that Ian's friend Mark had parents who were kind enough to go away to Greece and leave him on his own. She knew her parents would insist on a relative coming to stay rather than leave Tess and Marie on their own. The barbecue should be great, and it was the perfect weather for it.

At seven o'clock, just as Tess was trying to decide which skirt to wear, the phone rang. With both parents out she had to answer it herself, and snatched up the phone impatiently. 'Yes?'

'Tess? I'm glad it's you! Listen, something dreadful has happened that I've got to tell you. I can't now, someone might be listening, but I'll give you the details tonight after I get back. I'll wait up for you if you're late.'

'What is it?' asked Tess, lowering her voice too before realizing there was no need. 'Marie, what's happened?'

'You won't believe it!' whispered Marie dramatically, and then her voice changed. 'Listen, You Know Who called in earlier and we've arranged to go out tomorrow night as I'm off work then. Could you and Ian arrange some kind of cover story for me? If I can't make it, I have to let him know in the next hour,' said Marie, her voice low and rushed.

'Like what?' demanded Tess.

'Anything! I thought you could have arranged something at this barbecue, and say we're both going out in a group. Natasha will be there, won't she? Say she invited me.'

'Well, all right, but why can't you make up your own stories?' demanded Tess. 'I don't see why I have to do it for you. I'm in the middle of changing, and to be honest I don't want—'

Marie's voice changed suddenly. 'I'm sorry, I'm afraid you've got the wrong number. This is the Skylark Motel,' she said briskly, and the receiver was replaced with a sharp click.

Tess stood with the dead receiver in her hand and wondered what could possibly have got Marie so worked up that she was willing to stay up until Tess got back that night in order to tell her about it. Since working at the motel Marie had insisted that she needed her sleep in order to cope, and usually fell straight into bed when she got back from the four to ten shift.

All the time she was dressing Tess continued to think about the conversation. Trust Marie to get centre stage even when she was working! Tess thought to herself. Sometimes she wished that she didn't have a sister— not often but occasionally, like tonight.

*   *   *

The barbecue turned out to be as good as Tess had hoped. Most of the crowd that she and Ian hung around with were there, and although they had fun, it didn't get out of hand. Once, one of Ian's mates had held a party while his parents were abroad and they'd been invaded by gatecrashers. Neighbours had called the police in. Thanks to some careful vetting by some of the group this didn't happen and for a few hours Tess forgot Marie's strange phone call. It was only when she and Ian were walking home that she remembered, and she repeated it word for word to him.

'Sounds like another of her ego trips,' commented Ian. 'I can't imagine waitresses get to find out anything very interesting, can you?'

'No, but she really sounded strange—excited but nervous too, if you know what I mean.'

'She was probably nervous about asking us to make up another story for her for tomorrow night,' said Ian irritably. 'I do wish you'd stand up to her sometimes, Tess. You never refuse her anything, even when it makes you feel miserable. She's using you, can't you see that? And do you think this guy of hers really is separated from his wife?'

Tess knew that but for Jean-Paul she would stand up to Marie more, but she didn't dare risk Ian finding out that she'd two-timed him. He was going away soon anyway, and nothing must be allowed to spoil their last weeks together. Resentment of her sister simmered inside her, giving her an actual pain in her stomach.

'Of course he is!' she replied. 'Marie says they've been separated for over two years now.'

'Perhaps he isn't telling Marie the truth.'

'I think Marie would know,' said Tess. 'Look, if you don't mind I'd like to go in now. She said she'd wait up for me and I can't wait to hear this incredible story of hers.'

Ian laughed. 'You'll probably find the reality a let-down. Give me a bell in the morning and let me know. I bet you I'm right.'

'How much?' asked Tess.

'No money,' called Ian as he walked away. 'I don't want to take advantage of your touching faith in your own sister!'

Smiling, Tess let herself into the house.

'Is that you, Marie?' called her mother.

Tess felt the smile slip from her face as she checked her watch and saw that it was nearly half past eleven. 'No, Mum, it's me. Isn't Marie in yet?'

Her father came to the door of the front room, an anxious frown on his normally placid features. 'No, she isn't,' he said shortly. 'Did she say anything to you about going out with Alec after work?'

'Alec?' asked Tess stupidly, her mind still on Marie's unknown boyfriend.

'Yes, Alec. He *is* her boyfriend at the moment, isn't he?'

Tess hoped she wouldn't blush. 'Sure. I wasn't thinking straight. No, she was coming straight home the last I

30

heard.'

'When did she tell you that?' asked her father.

'She rang about half-past seven, just before I went out.'

'Why?' asked her mother.

Tess hesitated. She couldn't mention the business of the date the following night, but the rest of the conversation sounded a bit weird on its own. 'I'm not sure,' she said at last. 'She couldn't talk for long because they're not meant to make personal calls from work, but she did say she'd stay up for me tonight.'

'Which means she should have been home by now,' said her father.

'Well, yes, but you know what Marie's like. She might have met up with someone and—'

'Do you have Alec's number?' asked her mother.

'We could call him.'

This was getting worse and worse, thought Tess, praying that Marie would walk in the door before much longer. 'Ian might have it, but I know Alec was out with someone else tonight,' she explained.

'Another girl?' asked her mother.

Tess sighed. 'I don't know,' she said. 'He might have been; it isn't as though he and Marie are engaged or anything.'

'No, but they've been spending an awful lot of time together,' her father pointed out. 'I think we should check with him. Ring Ian for his number, would you, Tess?'

'I'll look him up in the book. I know where he lives,' said Tess, desperate to keep Ian out of the mess Marie had landed them all in.

Just as she'd known it would, the call, which was taken by Alec's mother, confirmed that Alec was out for the evening with a girlfriend.

'That's that then,' said Tess's mother, trying not to look too worried. 'We'll just have to wait a bit longer.'

Tess made herself a sandwich, took a Coke from the fridge and then carried her supper up to her room. The last thing she wanted was to sit with her parents and face one of their inquisitions. Silently she cursed Marie for putting her in this position in the first place, and then cursed herself for allowing Marie to use her the way she had.

'Never again, Marie,' she muttered fiercely. 'From now on you're on your own.'

But as the minutes ticked away Tess's anger began to change to fear, and at twelve o'clock she went downstairs. Her father was on the phone to the local police station giving a description of Marie. Suddenly Tess felt sick.

'They've taken down the details but want us to ring again if she still isn't back by three a.m.,' he said as he hung up.

'Three!' exclaimed Tess. 'Why don't they start looking now?'

'Because lots of teenage girls don't come home at the time they say they will, and I had to tell him that Marie once stayed out all night.'

'But that was different,' said Tess. 'She'd been to a party and couldn't get a lift home.'

'She did have a telephone in the house,' he said wearily.

'Yes, but they'd been—'

'Drinking, I know that. It doesn't make any difference, Tess. She's let us down once and he's probably right. She'll come waltzing in through the door any minute now and ask us what we were in such a state about.'

'They are taking it seriously though, aren't they?' asked Tess.

'They'll give the description to the patrol car drivers straight away. Anything else will have to be put on hold for a few hours.'

Tess decided she didn't want to know what 'anything else' was. She felt as though someone had caught hold of her stomach and knotted it into a tight ball, and it was an effort to breathe normally as anxiety tightened her chest.

'Ring the motel,' she said suddenly. 'Make sure she left on time.'

'We've already done that, before you got back,' said her mother. 'Her shift ended a little bit late but the receptionist saw her leave at ten-thirty.'

Tess turned away and walked back up to her room. 'Come home quickly, Marie,' she whispered to herself. 'Just come home safely and I'll never

34

complain about you again, not even to Ian.' She then knelt on her bed and looked down the road, willing the slim figure of Marie to come into sight beneath the street lamp on the corner, but at three o'clock in the morning Marie had still not returned.

CHAPTER THREE

At four a.m. Tess and her parents were sitting in their front room together with a young WPC and an older male police sergeant. It was the sergeant who did most of the talking while the WPC took notes and added the odd question. Both were calm and sympathetic, their manner reassuring, but Tess knew that this wasn't helping her parents any more than it was helping her. It was quite clear now that something had happened to Marie.

'You say you've tried the local hospital?' queried Sergeant Wilkinson.

Tess's father nodded. 'I rang them again just before you arrived. No one answering to Marie's description has been brought in tonight.'

The policeman nodded. 'Try not to worry, Mr Phillips,' he said quietly. 'I know it looks bad to you right now, but believe me, we see a lot of this in our job. Isn't that right, Deborah?' The WPC nodded and smiled across at Tess. Tess didn't smile back—she couldn't. Her lips felt frozen, unable to move in even an attempt at a smile.

'You'd be surprised how often this happens,' the WPC agreed, tucking her pencil into the spine of her notebook. 'You did say she finds it boring here?' she added as she reached the door.

'Well, yes,' said Tess, 'but like I said she was definitely coming home tonight. She wanted to tell me this incredible piece of news. It wouldn't make sense to call and say she'd wait up for me, and then just take off.'

'Don't you see? It could have been part of an elaborate plan,' said Sergeant Wilkinson. 'To keep us looking here while she went off to London.'

'No, I don't think so,' said Tess. 'If

Marie was going to run off to London she'd have told me. She'd never just leave like this.' But in her heart she wasn't sure. Perhaps Marie had been protecting her again, for her own good.

The sergeant and the WPC glanced at each other and then back at Tess and her parents. 'You'd be surprised what young people do. It isn't that they want to upset you, they simply don't think. Now, we'll get everything underway at the station, but if she calls you, ring us at once, won't you?'

Tess's father stood up. 'Of course we will, but Tess is right. Marie isn't the kind of girl who'd vanish without a word.'

'Anyway,' said Tess's mother, scrunching a handkerchief between her fingers, 'she'd never have left her boyfriend. They've been going steady together for weeks now. Isn't that right, Tess?'

The WPC was glancing in her notebook to check Alec's name and address, and missed the crimson tide of colour that washed over Tess's face and neck, but the sergeant noticed. 'Is there something you haven't told us?' he asked softly. 'You can always have a chat with us privately if you like.'

Tess shook her head. 'There's nothing, honestly.'

'Of course there isn't,' said her mother, fiercely. 'We've told you about Marie staying out that time, and now and again we have had a bit of trouble with her, but Tess has never given us a moment's worry and she wouldn't tell lies at a time like this. Why don't you get back to the station and start looking for Marie?' she added, her voice beginning to break with the strain.

They apologized, went to the front door with Tess's father and continued talking to him in low voices while Tess sat frozen on the sofa, her mother's hand on her shoulder, wishing that she could vanish like Marie. She knew that soon, very soon, she was going to have to tell everyone about her sister's secret boyfriend and the knowledge was like a heavy weight in the middle of her chest.

'Try and get some rest, darling,' said

her mother as the front door closed behind the police. 'We'll wake you if there's any news.'

Tess went up to her room but she couldn't sleep, and at seven o'clock she phoned Ian and asked him to come round so that he could be with her when she told her parents the truth.

'You mean you haven't told them yet?' he asked in astonishment.

'I just couldn't say it,' confessed Tess miserably. 'It was awful having the police here and everything, and I know the parents will totally freak out when they know.'

'Not half as much as the police will freak out when they find you've been lying to them,' responded Ian.

'Stop it!' shouted Tess. 'You're meant to be on my side.'

'Sorry, it's only that it makes me mad to think of the trouble Marie's caused you with her lies and cover-ups.'

'I don't care about getting into trouble,' said Tess vehemently. 'All I care about is seeing Marie again. Where is she, Ian? What do *you* think has happened to her?'

'I've no idea, but I'll come straight over, then we can tell your parents the truth and they can pass it on to the police. That way you won't have all this on your conscience any longer.'

'Thanks,' said Tess gratefully.

Fifteen minutes later Ian was at the front door and Tess let him in quietly. She'd hoped for a chance for a few words with him before they told her parents, but the moment he walked in the front door her father came out of the kitchen into the hall and she knew that was the end of that.

'Ian, what are you doing here so early?' he asked quickly. 'Have you got some news about Marie?'

Ian shook his head. 'I'm sorry, Mr Phillips, but no, at least no news about where she is. There is something that Tess and I think you should know though.'

Mr Phillips took one look at their solemn faces and fetched his wife to join them in the front room where only a few hours earlier they'd been talking to the police.

'Right then, what's this all about?' he

asked.

Once again Tess sat upright on the sofa, her hands clenched in her lap. Now it was her parents she was facing rather than the police. At least this time she had the comfort of Ian's arm round her shoulders.

'It's about Marie and Alec,' she mumbled.

'Marie and what?' asked her mother anxiously.

'Alec!' Tess's voice came out in a nervous shout and she rushed on before she lost her nerve completely. 'Marie and Alec aren't going steady, it's a casual arrangement. They both go out with other people as well.'

'But, why did you tell us ... ?' Her mother's red-rimmed eyes were puzzled.

'Marie asked all of us—that's me, Ian and Alec—to help give her a cover story.'

'What was she covering up?' asked her father grimly.

Tess felt Ian's arm tighten round her and she swallowed hard. 'Well, she'd got this new guy, but his divorce hadn't come through yet and she knew you wouldn't approve.'

'What's his name?' demanded her father angrily, while her mother continued to look puzzled.

'I don't know,' explained Tess. 'She never told me.'

'You mean to say that Marie's been running around with a married man for months now and you lied for her without knowing who he was?' Her father sounded both shocked and hurt by the deception and Tess wanted to cry.

'I did try,' she protested. 'Marie wouldn't talk about it.'

'Why did you lie for her, Tess?' asked her mother. 'Don't you see, she couldn't have managed if it hadn't been for you?'

'I know, only—'

'But for you she might be here right now,' said her father furiously.

'No!' protested Tess, turning her head into Ian's shoulder in an attempt to hide her tears.

'I don't think that's fair, Mr Phillips,' said Ian quickly. 'You know how forceful Marie can be and—'

'I'm phoning the police station immediately,' retorted Mr Phillips. 'I think you should leave, Ian. You'd better warn your friend Alec that the police will be on their way to see him, if they haven't been already. Now he'll have to explain this cover-up to them himself.'

Ian didn't want to leave Tess, but he knew that he couldn't stay if he wasn't wanted. Anyway, the tense atmosphere in the house made him very uncomfortable. 'I'll ring you later,' he promised Tess as he left.

Soon after Mr Phillips' call a police car pulled up outside the house again and Tess had to tell her story once more. She was horrified to discover that even when she'd gone over it twice they didn't seem to believe her. The WPC took her into the kitchen for a chat, leaving the sergeant with her parents. 'Where did you say you and your boyfriend were last night?' she asked.

'At a barbecue; I gave you the address.'

'And this Alec wasn't there?'

'No.'

'Where was he?'

Tess shrugged. 'I've no idea. Out with a girlfriend somewhere.'

'Do you know the girlfriend's name?'

'No, but I'm sure he does,' said Tess, who didn't understand why the police weren't more concerned about the married man.

'How do you know he was with a girlfriend?' persisted the WPC.

'Alec's mother told us when we rang last night.'

'Alec says he was on his own,' said the policewoman, watching Tess carefully.

Tess frowned. 'On his own? Alec's never on his own!'

The policewoman wrote this down in her notebook and immediately Tess wished she'd kept quiet. No matter what she said she seemed to be making everything worse at the moment. 'Has anyone seen Marie since she left the Skylark?' she asked despairingly.

'I'm afraid not, but we're concentrating our search on the area around there, and along the route she usually took home. So far no one's come forward to say they saw her. Tess, is there anything you haven't told us, anything you didn't want to say in front of your parents?'

'Like what?' asked Tess in bewilderment.

'Was Marie in any kind of trouble?'

'What sort of trouble?'

The policewoman leant towards her in a friendly manner. 'She wasn't pregnant, was she?'

'No!' exclaimed Tess. 'Of course not.'

'Or not to your knowledge.'

Tess shook her head. 'You really don't understand anything about Marie. She'd have told me if there'd been anything like that, because it would have been such a disaster for her. All she wanted to do was get away from here, and if she'd been pregnant that would have been the end of her dreams.'

The WPC nodded and sat up straight again. 'Tess, I really do think that your sister's made off for the big city. I know you don't want to believe it, but it's the most likely explanation for her disappearance.'

'I'd rather believe that than anything worse,' muttered Tess.

'Look, I've got to go now, but if you want to talk to me about anything, however trivial, that relates to your sister then here's the number to ring. We're on the same side, you know, and holding back information doesn't help Marie, it just hinders us.'

Tess bit on her lower lip and nodded. She knew that, just as she knew with absolute certainty that Marie would never have taken off for any big city without telling her first.

'There is one thing,' she said before the policewoman had walked out of the door. 'Suppose that what she was telling me about over the phone was important to someone else—you know, dangerous?'

'I think that your sister was playing out some little drama to liven up life here in Stamfield,' said the WPC. 'Honestly, Tess, I don't think you should set too much importance by that particular conversation. She was probably on a break and feeling bored. Maybe she was going to have a laugh about you believing her when you got home.'

'She wasn't like that!' cried Tess. 'Why won't you listen to me? Marie didn't always tell the truth, but that was more by keeping things back than making them up.'

'Try and get some rest,' advised the WPC. 'You look exhausted.'

Tess wondered how she was expected to rest until Marie was found.

*   *   *

'What do you mean, the police didn't believe you?' Ian asked Alec as they sat on a park bench while Alec ate his midday sandwiches during his half-hour break from the garage.

'Exactly what I say. You see, I was meant to be meeting Marie last night. I waited on the main road, at the end of the lane that leads from the motel, but she never showed up. After half an hour I decided I'd been stood up again so I took my new motorbike out for a spin along the top road and then brought it back here and did some tuning work in the garage. I'm allowed to do that—it's why I've got a set of keys. Trouble is, no one saw me. The police aren't at all happy.'

'That's stupid,' said Ian. 'Suppose you had gone out with her, what do they think you've done with her now?'

Alec turned his dark blue eyes on Ian. 'Killed her, I guess.'

Ian felt a shiver run up the back of his neck. 'They think Marie's dead?' he whispered.

'That's the impression they gave me.'

'But they told Tess's family they were sure she'd run off. And what about her real boyfriend? Aren't they going to try and find out who he was?'

Alec sighed. 'They said they're asking around, but I didn't get the impression they were trying too hard. Mind you, I could be wrong. Most of the time they were probably putting pressure on me to see if I'd change my story.'

'It's all such a mess,' said Ian. 'If only

Marie hadn't been so secretive about this guy.'

'She must have had her reasons,' said Alec shortly. 'I wish I hadn't got involved, but you know what I'm like and I really fancied her. I thought that if this new guy faded from the scene she and I might become an item, and believe me, she was worth waiting for. Marie could really turn a guy on, and when she was with you she always made you feel that you were the one who mattered. She had this way of looking at you, giving you all her attention. It was very flattering.'

'Don't talk about her in the past,' said Ian quickly. 'I don't believe she's dead; that's too horrible to contemplate. The police might well be right, she was always moaning about being bored. She'll most likely ring Tess from London and say how great the big city is.'

Alec shook his head. 'I don't believe that. I'm more interested in the phone call you say she made to Tess yesterday afternoon. That has to have something to do with her disappearance. It might

49

also explain why I was left hanging around on my own, and ended up with no alibi.'

'I suppose we've got to rely on the police turning up a lead,' said Ian, after a short silence.

'I suppose so,' said Alec, pulling a face. 'They were far too interested in me for my liking, though.'

As they walked out of the park on their way back to the garage two police cars went speeding by, their sirens wailing, and the boys looked at each other with a mixture of hope and fear.

'Perhaps they've found something,' said Ian.

'If they have we'll soon know,' Alec assured him.

*   *   *

A few hours later they did know. The police had found something, but it wasn't Marie. Having failed to find any trace of her along the route from the Skylark Motel to her home they'd extended their search out into the fens and there they'd discovered a badly mutilated male corpse. Suddenly Stamfield stopped being the boring place Marie had complained about, as reporters and television cameras descended on the town to talk to people who knew the missing girl and to try to get any information they could on the newly found body.

'I wish the wretched man had chosen a different time to be killed!' Tess exclaimed to Ian that evening as they sat in her bedroom. 'Some of the police have had to come off Marie's case and go over to the murder.'

Ian caught hold of her hand. 'I'm sure that's not true. They've probably drafted in extra help from other forces. They're still searching for Marie, you know they are.'

'It's so horrible sitting around waiting for something to happen,' said Tess. 'And then you don't know what it will be. If the phone rings we all turn white, if the police call to give us an update we fear the worst, and the rest of the time I just sit looking out of the window waiting for her to come round the corner.'

Ian didn't know what to say. He could imagine only too well how dreadful it must be, and there was nothing he could do to help. 'I saw Alec at lunch time,' he said at last. 'He was pretty low as well.'

'Why?' asked Tess.

'Because he was meant to meet Marie on the night she disappeared. He waited around, then assumed she'd stood him up and took off on his motorbike. No one saw him, so he hasn't got an alibi.'

'Why does he need an alibi?' asked Tess.

'Without one, how do the police know Alec and Marie didn't meet up? And if they did, then he was the last person to see her, but isn't admitting it.'

'Why would Alec want to hurt Marie?' asked Tess. 'He doesn't have a motive.'

Ian shrugged. 'I've no idea; perhaps they think they quarrelled or she chucked him. Let's be honest, Tess. Marie did use Alec, and he might have got annoyed with her.'

Tess's eyes widened. 'What are you saying? That *you* believe Alec did something to Marie? He's your friend! You can't think he'd hurt her so badly that ...' Her voice tailed off. She couldn't bring herself to say any more.

'Of course not!' protested Ian. 'I'm just saying it's not unreasonable of the police to be a bit suspicious.'

'But they don't know Marie often stood him up, unless you told them.'

Ian frowned. 'I haven't told them anything about Alec and Marie. You're the only person I've discussed this with.'

'You don't like Marie, do you?' asked Tess softly.

Ian looked irritated. 'Sure I do, but I don't like her influence over you. I know she's good fun at parties, and like Alec said to me today she has a knack of making people feel special when she's talking to them, but that's surface stuff. She doesn't really care about anyone except herself, and that's why it's going to be hard to find her. I don't think any of us, not even you, Tess, really know Marie.'

'You may be right,' admitted Tess in a low voice. 'I have a feeling that the police aren't going to find out what's happened to Marie. Let's face it, the first twenty-four hours are vital and so far they haven't got a single clue. The more time that passes the harder it will be for them to find physical evidence of anything.'

'I know what you mean, but what happens if you're right?' asked Ian. 'You and your parents can't spend your lives waiting for the phone to ring or a knock on the door—you'd all go mad.'

'If I'm right,' said Tess firmly, 'and they try to tell us that Marie's simply bunked off like hundreds of other girls before her then we're going to have to find out what happened ourselves.'

'You and me?' asked Ian.

'And Alec,' said Tess quickly. 'Working at the garage he meets far more people than we do. Everyone gossips there when they're buying their papers and paying for petrol, and if he's under suspicion himself he'll certainly want to clear his name.'

Ian wasn't sure and tried to explain

54

why to Tess. 'The police are used to this kind of thing, Tess. They know what happens and what to look for. They won't just let it go.'

'No, but Marie will become a statistic, an officially listed "missing person", and that's not right. She isn't just a statistic, she's my sister, and I'm going to find her, even if I have to do it on my own.'

'You won't have to do it on your own,' promised Ian. 'Of course I'll help, and I'm sure Alec will too, but right now we don't know it will be necessary.'

Tess stared out of her bedroom window into the street, now full of reporters and photographers all hungry for information. 'I know,' she said softly. 'I'd like to be wrong, but I'm not. You wait and see.'

Ian looked at her in surprise, and a chill touched him. He wondered how she could be so sure.

CHAPTER FOUR

Two weeks later there was still no sign of Marie, and Ian was forced to admit that Tess's prediction had been right. The police, with one definite murder on their hands following the discovery of the body in the fens, decided that unless any further information came to light Marie would be classified as a 'missing person'.

'Have you even considered the fact that there might be a link between this man's murder and my daughter's disappearance?' Mr Phillips asked Sergeant Wilkinson on one of his visits.

'Of course we've considered it,' the sergeant assured him, 'but the dead man isn't local, and without going into details the way he was murdered has led our officers along quite a different line of inquiry. A missing teenager doesn't fit the picture we're coming up with. Not that we're anywhere near to arresting anyone,' he added gloomily. 'My superiors are pressing for results.'

'And in the meantime Marie gets pushed to one side, does she?' asked Tess furiously.

'We'll continue to keep the inquiry going for some time yet,' Sergeant Wilkinson assured her. 'It's just that it has to be scaled down. Several diners at the motel remember Marie serving them at dinner at ten-fifteen that night and the receptionist saw her leave, alone, at ten-thirty. After that there's nothing. No sighting, no trace, just nothing. It's as though she stepped out of that motel entrance and disappeared into thin air.'

'Only she couldn't have done,' Tess pointed out.

The sergeant sighed. 'We know that, but you have to understand that there's no evidence of any crime. We've talked to a great many people and failed to come up with even the faintest of leads, which makes us suspect that we were right in the first place and Marie's taken off for the bright lights of one of the big cities. We've had confirmation of her ambitions in that direction during our inquiries, although I'm not at liberty to divulge the exact source.'

'And the boyfriend?' asked Tess. 'The mystery man who was meant to be getting a divorce?'

'Again, no one's seen her with any man lately. The only positive sighting we've had is when she was with you and your friends at the Burger King. It's always possible that the man didn't exist, you know,' he added gently.

Tess was angry. 'You mean that Marie lied about a boyfriend, for no reason that I can think of, and then lied again when she rang me up and said she had something incredible to tell me? Why? Why would she suddenly start lying?'

'We think,' said Deborah, the friendly WPC, 'that these lies are all indications that she was bored. She was trying to liven things up by making out her life was more exciting than it really was, but in the end she realized it wasn't getting her anywhere and so she made her move.'

Tess shook her head in disbelief and gave up listening as the conversation with her parents continued. She knew that the police were wrong, that it hadn't happened like that, because she knew Marie and they didn't. The new guy in her life had mattered to Marie. She'd always been anxious to look her best when she was meeting him and there'd been a glow about her when she'd returned from seeing him. Also, although Tess had kept this to herself, there were several items of expensive clothing in Marie's wardrobe that she wouldn't have been able to afford. No, there had been a man, and something dreadful had happened to her to stop her coming home, but clearly it was going to be up to Tess to find out what.

She, Ian and Alec met up that evening at Alec's house. They went out in the back garden where Alec was working on yet another motorbike, this time belonging to a friend.

'What can we do?' asked Tess, after she'd reported the afternoon's conversation between the police and her family. 'We can't let it go and sit around waiting to hear something. We must find out what's happened to Marie. Just suppose she's alive somewhere and waiting for the police to rescue her. What will she think as the days go by?'

Privately Alec didn't believe that Marie was alive any more, but he kept the thought to himself. He knew that there was a faint possibility that she might have gone to London but, like Tess, he had a gut feeling that the answer was more sinister than that. 'I'm going to try and raise the subject with some of the customers,' he said. 'After all, most of the males in this town end up at our garage, even if they only come in for petrol. One of them has to know something about Marie's boyfriend.'

'If only we knew someone who worked at the Skylark Motel, they could help us,' said Ian. 'She was there when she made that phone call to Tess, which means she most likely saw something, or someone, there that amazed her. The trouble is, we don't know a soul.'

'I want to find out the identity of the married guy she was seeing,' said Tess. 'The police can't have spoken to

60

everyone. Someone knows who he is—they must do.'

'Ask her friends,' suggested Alec. 'Talk to the girls from her art course. Chances are she dropped a few hints about him, if only to impress.'

'Good idea,' agreed Tess. 'I'll start tomorrow.'

'Be careful,' said Alec gently. 'If this unknown man is involved in her disappearance it could be dangerous if he gets to hear about your enquiries.'

Tess was surprised by the look of concern in his normally rather stern blue eyes. 'Don't worry,' she assured him, 'I'll be tactful and discreet.'

Ian laughed. 'If you are it will be the first time! You usually come straight out with what you want to say. That's one of the things I've always liked about you.'

'This is different,' Tess pointed out. 'What about you, Ian? What will you do?'

'Concentrate on the motel, but right now I'm not sure how to set about it.'

*　　　*　　　*

Ian was lucky. The following day Alec arrived at the garage and found that he was needed to work on a badly damaged Jaguar whose passenger door had been smashed in and the windscreen shattered by vandals.

He worked from eight in the morning until five at night and knew that it would be at least another day before the car was ready but at least it was looking better than when he started. He was about to lock up for the night when a tall, well-built man wearing a smart grey suit crossed the garage forecourt.

'Hi! I'm Keith Palmer, owner of the Jaguar you've got in for repair. How's it going?' he asked.

'Be another day at least,' replied Alec, trying to remember who Keith Palmer was. He didn't have to think about it for long.

'Can't you make it by mid-afternoon tomorrow?' queried Keith. 'I'm busy up at the motel and need my car.'

'I'll do my best,' promised Alec, deciding it might be useful to get on the right side of the man. 'I could always put in some overtime if it's really urgent.'

'I'd make it worth your while,' promised Keith. 'It's the kind of car that spoils you for driving others.'

'I can imagine. Do you want to see what I've done so far?' added Alec.

'Sure,' agreed Keith and together they went into the repair area.

'How's business at the motel?' asked Alec casually as Keith Palmer walked round his car, examining the bodywork on the dented passenger side carefully.

'Trade's good but I can't keep staff. That's the trouble with youngsters today—no staying power.'

Alec was tempted to say that Marie seemed to have possessed vanishing power, but he kept quiet, sensing a way of getting Ian inside the motel itself. 'What kind of staff do you need?' he asked.

'It's the waiters in the lounge/coffee room area who keep leaving. They don't like the shift work and are either bored at the slow times or rushed off their feet when we're busy. No pleasing them, it seems. You've done a good job on the car so far.'

'Thanks,' acknowledged Alec. 'You know,' he added slowly, trying to keep his voice casual, 'I've got a friend who wants work at the moment. He's waiting for his A-level results before taking off abroad. He did apply to the motel but there were no vacancies for men then. Could he apply for a job as a waiter?'

'How old is he?'

'Eighteen. I've known him for years, we were at secondary school together. He wouldn't let you down, he's an OK guy.'

'If he's as good at waiting at tables as you are with cars I'll certainly have no quarrel with him,' said Keith, patting his car affectionately. 'Sure, tell him to ring the motel and ask for an interview. What's his name? I'll make a note of it and tell our personnel department to give him a try.'

'It's Ian, Ian Groves,' said Alec, trying hard to conceal his excitement.

'OK, that's a deal. You get my car done by mid-afternoon tomorrow and

I'll give your friend a two week trial at the motel. Can't say fairer than that, can I?'

'You're on,' promised Alec, although how he was going to get the Jaguar ready for the road by then he had no idea, unless he worked half the night.

'See you at four tomorrow,' called Keith, walking briskly away and climbing into a black Renault 19.

As soon as he'd gone Alec sprinted to the nearest public telephone box and rang Ian to give him the good news.

'Make sure you get the car done!' said Ian. 'What a stroke of luck!'

'Yeah, well, you be careful too. Someone at the Skylark might have something they want to hide. Be careful and don't go blundering in asking questions the moment you arrive.'

'I do have a brain of my own,' retorted Ian.

'Half a brain!' laughed Alec, before hanging up.

*   *   *

By working every possible moment Alec was able to get the Jaguar repaired on time and, true to his word, Keith Palmer arranged for Ian to be taken on as a waiter at the Skylark Motel, at first working the ten to six shift in the lounge bar.

Ian arrived for work on his first day feeling very apprehensive. He wasn't too worried about the job, although he did wonder how he'd get on carrying loaded trays to and from the kitchen, but he was concerned about how he could bring up the subject of Marie.

During his first short morning break he found himself drinking a cup of coffee in the staff room along with a waitress called Karen, who worked in the dining room, just as Marie had done.

'How's it going then?' she asked him, her eyes faintly amused.

'Fine, thanks.'

Karen raised her eyebrows. 'You mean you haven't got a complaint yet? Just wait! It won't be long before the customers—or guests as we're meant to call them—start getting up your nose. They can be horribly rude, especially the coffee morning ladies. No one lasts long in your job.'

'What about in yours?' asked Ian. 'I guess the waitresses come and go pretty quickly too.'

Karen shook her head. 'Not really. The hours are a pain but you get good tips. No, most of us have been here since the place opened.'

'Didn't that local girl—I forget her name—go missing from here?' asked Ian.

Karen looked round nervously. 'We're not encouraged to talk about that,' she said softly. 'It's done us a lot of harm having the police around asking questions. Mr Palmer's forbidden us to gossip about it. He's afraid it will put the customers off. The atmosphere here has to be relaxing.'

'I can see his point. Did you know her at all?'

She pulled a face. 'Not really; Marie wasn't the kind of girl you ever got to know, she kept herself to herself. At least as far as the other waitresses went she did.'

Ian had the feeling that despite Karen's first statement he could have pursued the subject, but decided that he didn't want to seem too interested yet and let it drop.

'It's my legs that hurt,' he told her with a rueful grin. 'Standing's more tiring than walking.'

Karen nodded. 'By the end of the night shift my shoes feel two sizes too small for my feet,' she told him. 'You get used to it though. Right—better get back. We only have ten minutes, you know.'

With a nod Ian returned to the coffee lounge. It was rapidly filling up with people who'd come for a lunch-time drink and bar snack and for the next three hours he was very busy. However, by three there were only two tables in use, and once he'd served the guests with their afternoon teas he found himself with nothing to do but stand behind the bar in his blue and yellow uniform trying to look alert.

'How's it going?' asked a voice from behind him. Ian turned round and saw

Keith Palmer standing in the room off the bar.

'Fine, thanks. We've been busy but as you can see there's a lull now.'

'That's the way it goes. Not planning on jacking it in, are you?'

Ian shook his head. 'No way! I need the money.'

Keith smiled. 'Don't we all! Your friend—what's his name? The one who works at the garage.'

'Alec.'

'Right, Alec. He's handy with cars.'

'I know. Cars and motorbikes have been his passion for as long as I've known him. He's never happier than when he's tinkering around with some engine or other.'

'Tell him from me he did a great job on my Jag.'

'I will,' promised Ian but as he watched Keith Palmer walk away he wondered what, if anything, he knew about Marie and whether or not he'd ever stood and chatted to her.

*　　　*　　　*

As Ian settled in to his first day at the motel, Tess began her task of talking to Marie's college friends. Several of them were abroad for some of the holiday but she knew that Annie, who like Marie hoped to go to London one day and work in the fashion industry, would be at home because her mother was housebound and during the holidays she took over some of the caring.

She went to her house and rang the front door bell. After a long wait the door was opened and a very harassed looking Annie stood in front of her, although when she saw it was Tess she managed a strained smile. 'Hi, Tess. How are you doing?'

'Not too badly,' said Tess in a low voice. 'It's pretty hard as you can imagine, but we're all coping.'

Annie hesitated a moment. 'Do you want to come in?' she asked at last. 'Mum's in bed, but we can have a chat in the kitchen as long as we don't make too much noise.'

'Thanks,' said Tess gratefully.

It was clear that Annie was no

housekeeper. The whole place was in chaos and there was a stack of ironing on the table which she quickly put on one of the worktops as they sat down. 'Sorry about all this. I'm utterly hopeless at getting organized but it does save some money if I take over from the women Dad pays when I can. It's an awful thing to say but I can't wait to get away from here.'

These familiar words made Tess's heart jump into her throat; she'd heard Marie say them so many times. 'Annie, do you think Marie's run off?' she asked bluntly, abandoning the subtle approach in the face of such an obvious opening.

Annie thought for a few minutes and then shook her head. 'No, I don't.'

'Why not? The police seem certain it's what's happened.'

'I don't think she'd have left her boyfriend. She was dead keen on him.'

'Who was he, Annie?' asked Tess urgently.

Annie sighed. 'I wish I knew. The police kept asking me that, and when I couldn't give them a name they implied they didn't believe her story. They seemed to think that it was Alec she was seeing all the time, but that's a load of rubbish. I told them how badly Marie treated Alec—you know, standing him up at the last minute. She'd laugh about that. This other guy was loaded. He was always buying her things: chocolates, flowers, clothes— you name it, Marie got it. She even had some jewellery but I've no idea where she kept it because she told me she wouldn't be able to take it home. I was always asking who he was, but she said if she told one person in a town this size it would be common knowledge within a week. She played it very safe.'

'Why doesn't he come forward and say who he is if he's got nothing to hide? That's what I'd like to know,' said Tess. 'He has to be involved in her disappearance—that's the only reason that makes sense.'

'I'm not so sure about that,' said Annie, lifting her head at the sound of a bell being rung upstairs. 'Look, I'll have to go up to Mum now, she needs me, but there is one thing I can tell you. I don't believe this guy, whoever he is, was even separated. I think he and Marie were having a fling on the side. He didn't want to put his marriage in danger then, and he doesn't now, which is why he's keeping silent.'

'But Marie thought he *was* separated, didn't she?'

Annie pushed back her chair and stood up. 'Sorry, Tess, you'll have to leave now.'

'She didn't know he was still married, did she? And come to that, nor do you.'

Annie shook her head. 'Tess, Marie could be very devious and sometimes I don't think any of us truly knew the real her.'

'I did—do,' Tess corrected herself quickly. 'I'm her sister.'

'OK then, for what it's worth here's what I think: I think Marie was having an affair with a married man and didn't care as long as no one found out.'

'Why? She was never going to be able to marry him.'

'No, but it made her feel powerful

and important and that mattered to Marie.'

'You're her friend!' exclaimed Tess as she went out the front door. 'You don't even sound as though you like her much.'

Annie stopped at the foot of the stairs. 'By the time she vanished I didn't. She went out with Mark last term and when I found out and we split up she dumped him. All she wanted was to show me that she could have him if she wanted. It wasn't important to her, but it was to me. So, I suppose you'd have to call me an ex-friend.'

Tess was shocked. 'She went out with Mark? *Your* Mark?'

'Right, only he isn't my Mark any more.'

'But she never said anything to me!'

'There you are then. That proves it, doesn't it?'

'Proves what?' asked Tess.

'That she didn't tell you everything. Sorry to disillusion you, Tess, but perhaps it will make your job easier if you know more about her.'

'What job?' asked Tess.

'This one. You're trying to find out what happened to her, aren't you?'

'Yes, because the police don't seem to care.'

'I wish you luck then. And be careful.'

'Why do you say that?'

'Because I like you, and in view of the fact that Marie's vanished I'd have thought what you were doing was pretty risky. See you around.'

The blue painted front door closed firmly behind her and Tess was left standing on the path feeling more than a little shaken and slightly sick. What she'd heard had revealed an entirely new side to her sister's character—a side Tess didn't like very much.

'Oh, Marie!' she murmured under her breath as she made her way to the next house on her list. 'What other games did you play that you kept to yourself?'

CHAPTER FIVE

That evening Tess and Ian went to a disco at the local sixth form college. They were half-hoping to get a chance to talk to some of Marie's friends. Normally they loved to dance but tonight they had other things on their minds.

'How did your day go?' asked Tess as they sat together in a quiet corner of the room, hands linked and shoulders resting comfortably against each other.

'Pretty well,' said Ian. 'I've already met one girl who worked with Marie, although we didn't discuss her much because it's obvious it's a forbidden topic at the place and I didn't want to push my luck this early on. I also met Keith Palmer, the owner. He was the man who gave Marie the job, wasn't he?'

'Yes. I remember that because I thought it was a bit odd the owner taking the trouble to interview prospective waitresses.'

'He seems all right. He had a quick word with me but I noticed he chatted more to the girls,' said Ian. 'Interviewing pretty ones for jobs is probably a perk for him!'

'Did you get to talk to the receptionist? The one who was the last person to see Marie on the night she vanished?' asked Tess anxiously.

'No, because there are several of them and they work different shifts from week to week, but I will. Considering it was my first day I think I did well even to bring up Marie's name.'

'I thought they'd all be talking about her,' said Tess, draining her Coke and tapping her foot to the music.

'Bad for business,' explained Ian. 'It puts the guests off when the police come round, or so Karen says.'

'Karen?'

'The waitress I mentioned.'

'Is she pretty?' asked Tess. 'Marie was sure she'd get the job on looks.'

'Stunning!' teased Ian, but then he relented. 'Don't be silly, Tess, I hardly noticed her. All I was interested in was what she knew. I've got you; why would I be looking for anyone else?'

'Mark had Annie but it didn't stop him,' said Tess, and she told Ian what had happened to Annie.

'I heard some gossip about him and Marie,' admitted Ian after she'd finished. 'What was your sister playing at?'

'Or Mark, come to that,' retorted Tess. 'He must have wanted to take her out. Some loyalty he showed! You aren't much better either—you never told me about it.'

'It was only gossip. Just the same I blame Marie more. She was always able to have any guy she wanted, so why choose Annie's?'

'Not *was*, is!' cried Tess. 'Don't talk about her as though she doesn't exist any more.'

'Sorry.' Ian put his arm round Tess and hugged her. 'Let's get out of here. We can have a walk and chat in private. People are looking at us here.'

'I wanted them to do more than just look,' muttered Tess as she stood up. 'I hoped someone would talk to us.

Maybe when they see how upset I am one of them will tell me who this mystery guy is.'

A few minutes later, when they were back at their table, a tall, red-haired girl came over. Tess remembered that she did art with Marie.

'Hi! I'm Sara,' she said awkwardly. 'I wanted to say, you know, how sorry I am. It must be awful not knowing what's happened to Marie.'

'Yes, it is,' said Tess. 'Have the police been to see you?'

Sara nodded. 'Three days ago.'

'Were you able to tell them anything helpful?' asked Tess eagerly.

Sara sat down next to her. 'I told them everything I knew, but I don't know if it was helpful or not.'

'What exactly did you say?' asked Ian softly.

'Well, it was about Alec. You see, Marie had told me only a few days before she vanished that Alec was becoming too possessive. She enjoyed playing the field, but he wanted them to go steady. Apparently he'd lost his temper the previous night when she

79

said she couldn't see him, and she told me she was going to chuck him. She knew I'd be interested because I fancy Alec like mad. At least, I did. I'm not so sure now. I don't like guys with bad tempers.'

'Did she say anything about her married boyfriend?' asked Tess, slightly stunned by what she'd already heard.

Sara frowned. 'The police asked me that, but I never heard Marie mention a married man.'

'Did you tell the police that too?' asked Ian.

Sara nodded. 'Yes, of course. I don't think they were surprised. Said something about Marie having a fantasy life.'

Tess could hardly believe her ears, and seeing her distress Sara quickly went back to her friends.

'I don't believe it!' said Tess despairingly. 'No wonder the police are dragging their heels. And what about Alec? Marie never told me he was possessive, and you said he was quite laid-back about the way she treated him.'

Ian stood up. 'I think your sister told different stories to different people to confuse everyone. If Sara had ever heard about a married boyfriend, she'd have told the police. It's another of Marie's games, but now she's vanished those games are getting in the way of the truth.'

'And Alec?' asked Tess as Ian guided her outside. 'Do you believe he got angry with Marie?'

'He has got a temper,' admitted Ian, 'but I don't think he would have quarrelled with Marie about other blokes. He'd just have stopped seeing her.'

'You don't sound sure,' said Tess slowly.

'I'm as sure as possible, but I can't *know*, can I? Look, let's go and see Alec. We'll try the garage first in case he's doing some unpaid overtime on a friend's machine, and if he's not there we'll call in at his home.'

*   *   *

Alec wasn't at the garage, and they only just caught him at home as he was on his way out to the newly opened nightclub, Take Four. It was the first time Tess had seen him dressed up—the nightclub didn't allow anyone in if they were wearing jeans—and she thought how handsome he looked in his black trousers, dark red grandad-style shirt and black waistcoat. She could understand why the girls fell over each other in their efforts to go out with him.

'Did you want anything special?' he asked them.

'Not really, only another view on what we've found out today,' said Ian.

Alec frowned. 'Look, I'm as keen as you are on discovering what's happened to Marie but I do have a life to lead as well. I'm busting myself at work trying to keep up with everything, the police are still dropping by for a "quick word", and just for this one evening I'd like to enjoy myself without thinking about Marie.'

'Sure, no problem,' said Ian, with a glance at Tess. They were both a bit startled by his friend's vehemence.

'If it was a motorbike that had vanished you'd keep looking until you found it,' said Tess furiously. 'What a pity it's a person! Dead boring, I suppose.'

Alec stared at her in surprise. 'Hey, back off! I didn't mean it like that.'

'You wanted to go steady with her,' said Tess accusingly. 'You were jealous of her other boyfriend, weren't you?'

Alec gave her a long, hard look. 'If you want to talk about Marie, can we make it tomorrow? Say half eight at my place?'

'Sure,' agreed Ian placatingly, putting a warning hand on Tess's arm. 'We'll be there. Have a good time.'

Alec smiled. 'I intend to!'

'He's so arrogant,' said Tess angrily as they walked back towards the town centre.

'He isn't,' said Ian. 'Alec's a good friend, which is more than can be said for your sister from what you've told me. Alec wouldn't steal my girlfriend, and he wouldn't lie to me either.'

'Really?' Tess turned to face him.

'Are you saying he wouldn't steal me out of loyalty, or are you saying he doesn't fancy me?'

Ian pulled Tess close to him and stroked the back of her head. 'Stop it, Tess. Just calm down. There's no point in us quarrelling, and you're not being fair to Alec either. He's agreed to help us, and but for him I wouldn't have a job at the Skylark. Don't be so impatient. This is going to take time.'

Tess, her head resting against his chest so that she could hear his steady heartbeat in her ear, knew that he was right. 'I'm sorry,' she said softly, 'only I'm afraid we don't have much time. I miss her so much. Every morning when I wake up I get this sinking feeling in my stomach when I remember that she's still missing, and if I'm not doing anything about finding her then I feel I'm letting her down.'

The pair of them moved into a shop doorway where they began to kiss, gently at first but then more passionately, and by the time Ian walked Tess home she was feeling a little better. She knew that Ian was right, and that it was bound to take time, but the waiting was very hard.

She let herself quietly into the house. The doctor had given her mother some pills to take at night, which meant that once she'd got off to sleep it was best not to wake her or she had trouble falling asleep again. To her surprise her father was standing in the hall waiting for her.

'What do you know about this?' he asked, holding out his right hand.

Tess stared at the expensive-looking diamond-studded watch lying in his palm and raised astonished eyes to his. 'Nothing. Why?'

'Because I found it in your room.'

'It isn't mine,' said Tess. 'I've never seen it before.'

'I went into your room to get a paperback for your mother to read. When I took one down from your bookshelf I accidentally dislodged everything and this fell out from behind the bookend. It was in a plain box.'

'Well, it's nothing to do with me,' said Tess. 'I've no idea who it belongs to or how it got there, but it isn't mine.'

Her father's face was pale with worry and fatigue. 'I didn't think it was,' he admitted. 'I've got a feeling this belongs to Marie.'

Tess knew that he was right, and that this time she had to be honest with him.

'I spoke to Annie Rogers today— she's in Marie's art class at college— and she told me that this mystery boyfriend gave Marie jewellery,' she said.

'Then why hide it in your room and not her own?'

'I suppose,' said Tess slowly, 'that it was a kind of insurance. If you'd learned about this guy and gone through her things trying to find out who he was, she didn't want you discovering his presents.'

'Does Annie know who he is?' asked Mr Phillips.

Tess shook her head. She'd felt exhausted before she got in. Having this thrust at her was the final straw. 'I'm really tired, Dad. I must go to bed,' she said apologetically, aware that he wanted to talk more.

'Yes, sorry; it's only that ...' He stopped, unable to discuss his missing daughter for fear of breaking down.

Tess stood on tiptoe and brushed her lips against his cheek. ''Night, Dad. I'm really sorry. I know how you feel. It's the same for me.'

'Goodnight, Tess.'

Once in her room Tess found that she wasn't just tired, she was angry as well—angry with Marie for using her room to hide the watch, and angry with her in other ways too. She hadn't only used Tess to help her cover her tracks, she'd used her by telling her lies. If Tess had known the man wasn't separated, that he was still living with his wife, she'd never have gone along with what Marie wanted, and Marie must have known that.

'Perhaps Annie's wrong,' she muttered to herself as she got into bed. 'Maybe this guy's away on holiday and that's why he hasn't come forward.' It was a comforting thought and helped her get off to sleep, but deep down she didn't really believe it.

The next morning Ian rang.

'Tess, I'm sorry but I won't be able to make it to Alec's place tonight. I've been asked to swap shifts and do the six to ten instead. That's better really. I'll meet more people who saw Marie on her last night there.'

'OK,' said Tess, her pulse quickening at the prospect of him making some progress. 'That's great. I'll go to Alec's on my own. If I don't have any luck with Marie's friends today then I'll need some ideas from him.'

'You sure about that? I know you're not keen on Alec.'

'He's all right—it's his passion for cars that drives me mad, not him. Call you in the morning.'

'Sure. Good luck today!'

'And you,' said Tess, replacing the receiver.

*   *   *

When Ian arrived at the motel at ten to six he saw that the car park, usually only half-full, was packed with cars.

'What is it? A wedding reception?'

he asked another of the waiters as he changed into his uniform.

The other waiter, a twenty-year-old Australian called Dennis, shook his head. 'No, another party of Mr Palmer's special guests. They'll eat in the private room at the back.'

'What special guests are these?' enquired Ian.

'I think it must be some kind of rotary club, or maybe the Masons. They turn up every week or so, usually about fifteen of them, and once the meal's been served no one's allowed in there. They value their privacy, but Masons do, don't they?'

'Are they local people?' asked Ian.

'More likely Londoners from their voices,' said Dennis. 'Ignorant lot too—they never leave a tip.'

When Ian walked out into the lounge bar he saw a group of smartly dressed men sitting in a circle round one of the tables and guessed that these were the people Dennis was talking about. They all wore dark suits and very white shirts with blue or grey ties, and were passing papers around among themselves as they talked earnestly in low voices.

One of them glanced in Ian's direction and raised his hand. 'You, waiter! We could do with some refills over here.'

'Of course, sir,' said Ian politely, making his way over to the table with a notepad and pencil in his hand.

'Three draught bitters, two malt whiskies, five lagers and five gin and tonics,' said the man.

'Three draught bitters, three malt whiskies . . .'

'Two whiskies, not three!' shouted the man, making Ian jump in surprise. 'What's the matter with you Stamfield people? It's a simple enough thing to do, take down a list of drinks, for God's sake!'

'Quiet, Chris,' said another man, slightly older and with greying dark hair. 'The young man made a mistake, that's all. We all make mistakes, don't we?' He looked about him, and to Ian's surprise one by one the other men dropped their eyes and nodded in agreement.

'Sorry about that, son,' continued the older man. 'Chris has had a difficult couple of days and his temper is on a short fuse. No offence taken, I hope?'

'Of course not, sir,' replied Ian. 'If you could just give me the order again?'

He did, and this time Ian got it right and quickly brought the full glasses to the table. The first man—the one who'd shouted and whose name was Chris—didn't look up, but all the others smiled and thanked him as though he'd accomplished a really difficult task rather than simply doing his job.

He retreated back behind the bar where Dennis was waiting. 'Bad luck,' he whispered sympathetically. 'I got them two weeks ago and that Chris chap was with them then. He turned on me too, and all because I forgot to put ice in his gin and tonic. Look, here comes Mr Palmer. Now he'll sit down and join them and in about five minutes they'll retreat to their private room.'

'I'm glad we don't have to serve

them there,' said Ian with feeling. 'I'd be terrified of spilling something.'

'The only time I've ever seen that Chris smile was the first time he came here,' went on Dennis. 'There was a gorgeous girl working as a waitress in the dining room and he kept giving her the eye as she walked through the lounge.'

Ian felt a flicker of excitement. 'Is she still here?' he asked eagerly.

Dennis laughed. 'Sorry, mate, you're out of luck. She left.'

'I thought most of the waitresses liked working here. Karen says they get very good tips.'

Dennis glanced across the lounge to where the group of men and Keith Palmer were sitting talking, but seeing that they weren't looking his way he moved closer to Ian. 'No one knows why she left,' he said in a low voice. 'In fact, she didn't leave at all, not in the normal way. She just vanished. Walked out of here one evening and disappeared. You must have read about it. Marie her name was—Marie Phillips.'

Ian nodded. 'Of course! I read all about it but I don't know the details. What was she like?'

'Didn't talk to her much myself. She saved her smiles for the customers, and Mr Palmer by all accounts.'

'Keith Palmer?' asked Ian in astonishment.

'So the other girls say. It didn't make her too popular with them either. Mind you, it might not be true. She was a real looker, which would have made her unpopular whatever she did. Most of the girls here are dogs.'

'Karen's quite nice,' protested Ian, anxious for the conversation to change direction before Keith Palmer or any of his friends overheard.

'Yeah, but engaged. Look out, here come some more customers.'

Later that night Ian was carrying some bottles of wine from the storeroom to the bar when he passed a door marked 'Private'. He could hear raised voices as he drew level and stopped to try and make out what was being said.

'It was a stupid thing to do and you

know it!' shouted one man.

Fascinated, Ian moved closer to the door and rested an ear against the oak panels. Suddenly he felt a hand on the back of his neck and he was so startled that he nearly dropped the bottles of wine he was carrying.

'What the hell do you think you're doing snooping round here?' asked a furious voice, and twisting free of the man's grip Ian turned and found himself face to face with a very angry Keith Palmer.

For a moment his mind went blank but he swiftly recovered himself. 'I thought they'd be needing some more wine,' he explained, showing Keith the bottles originally destined for the bar. 'I knocked but didn't hear any reply so I knocked again and was trying to hear if they'd answered this time.'

For a very long moment Keith Palmer stared at him, and his usually friendly eyes were hostile. Then, after he'd studied Ian's innocent face he seemed to decide that his fears were groundless and his expression became amiable again.

'Didn't anyone tell you? These private parties don't need wine waiters. They're business seminars and the people prefer not to be interrupted.'

'Sorry,' said Ian. 'I didn't realize.'

'Not your fault, son. No point in taking those back to the storeroom though. Put them in the bar—they'll be needed there soon enough.' As he spoke he moved Ian slowly along the corridor towards the bar and away from the small private room.

'Right,' agreed Ian, and hurried away. When he put the bottles down in the bar he found that his hands were shaking and his legs felt weak. For one brief moment there'd definitely been something frightening about Keith Palmer.

*　　　*　　　*

When his shift ended Ian was thankful to leave, but on the way out he realized that there was a new receptionist on the desk. She was a pretty auburn-haired girl with a friendly smile and he wandered over to her.

95

'Quite busy tonight,' he remarked. 'It's my first night shift. Is it always like this?'

'No, it varies. In the lounge bar, are you?'

'That's right,' said Ian cheerfully. 'I was warned it's hard work but I quite like it.'

'Good.' The girl glanced back down at her pad and after a quick look round to make sure they were alone Ian took his chance. 'You're not the receptionist who was the last person to see that missing girl who worked here, are you?' he asked.

She raised her head and frowned at him. 'No, I'm not, and what's it to you anyway?'

'Nothing. I was just curious. Aren't you curious? After all, it's pretty odd that the police can't find any trace of her from the moment she left here.'

'You talked to Karen about that girl—I heard you in the canteen. I don't know why you're so interested. I don't think it's odd. If she had any sense she'd have caught the first train out of this boring town and good luck to her, that's what I say. As soon as I've saved up enough money I'll do the same. I moved here with my family last year and I've never been so bored in my life.'

'There are things to do,' said Ian with a smile. 'You'll have to let me show you around some time.'

She looked a little brighter. 'Sounds neat.'

'What's your name?' persisted Ian.

'Elaine. They gave me the wrong name badge—it said Eve—which is why I'm not wearing one, although I'm meant to. I mean, what's the point in wearing someone else's name badge? Stupid if you ask me.'

'Who's Eve? Does she work on the nights you don't?'

Elaine sighed. 'No, Eve's left. She left a couple of weeks ago. I guess she was the last person to see that waitress, but I might be wrong. I've never met her.'

'Why did she leave?' asked Ian urgently.

Elaine looked surprised at his interest in the departed Eve. 'Probably got fed up.'

'I guess so. See you then,' said Ian as he walked towards the front doors. Somehow, he thought, he had to find Eve and talk to her.

CHAPTER SIX

While Ian had been busy at the motel, Tess had spent the evening at Alec's house. His mood had improved and he even apologized about the night before.

'Sorry I was off with you,' he said with a disarming smile. 'I'd promised to meet someone outside Take Four and if you get there too late they don't let you in, because of the restriction on numbers.'

'Wouldn't she have been very pleased?' asked Tess laughingly.

'No way. Not that it matters; we won't be seeing each other again now.'

'Why not? Or shouldn't I ask?'

'It wasn't a big deal. She's fed up with me spending so much time at the garage anyway. Can't say I blame her, but you know what I'm like about cars and motorbikes. Besides, we've had a lot of extra work on recently and some of the time I'm working paid overtime.'

'Yeah, but most of the time you're not,' said Tess.

'True. What did you and Ian want to see me about?'

'We were going to bring you up to date on our progress so far and see if you'd heard anything at work.'

'Nothing at all. What about you though?'

'Well, on his first night, Ian talked to a waitress who'd known Marie but he didn't want to seem too interested so it was only a brief chat. I talked to Annie Rogers because I thought she might know who Marie's boyfriend was.'

'And did she?' asked Alec with interest.

'No, but she was quite certain that he wasn't separated, or even intending to get a divorce. She didn't think Marie cared either. Also, she told me this guy gave Marie lots of gifts, including jewellery which she was worried about taking home.'

'Anything else?' asked Alec.

Tess hesitated. 'She thought Marie treated you badly,' she admitted. 'She didn't like the way Marie would stand you up at the last minute.' She watched Alec's reaction carefully.

He was silent for a moment, then gave a harsh laugh. 'Nice of her to be concerned! I'm not saying I liked it. Sometimes I got totally fed up, but I'm no saint. I haven't always treated girlfriends too well, and when Marie and I did go out it was always an evening to remember! When we didn't, I saw other girls or worked on a car. Did Annie tell the police Marie treated me badly?'

'Well, yes,' admitted Tess.

He scowled. 'No wonder they won't get off my back.'

Tess nearly told him what Sara had said at the disco, but his frown was so ferocious that she lost her nerve. She kept remembering that he had no alibi for the night Marie vanished.

'Annie was certainly right about the jewellery,' she said, and then went on to

100

tell him about the watch her father had found in her room and how beautiful it was.

'That's a rotten thing to do,' said Alec, looking genuinely shocked. 'She should have had the guts to hide it in her own room, not used yours.'

'I suppose she thought if trouble broke Mum and Dad might well go through her things trying to find out who he was, but they'd never have thought of searching mine.'

'Do your parents do things like that?'

Tess shook her head. 'They never have; they're pretty strong on privacy and everyone's right to a private life, but I think a married boyfriend might have been a bit too much for them.'

'Have you found out anything today?' asked Alec, pouring them both two glasses of Coke from a litre bottle and then guiding Tess through into a large, comfortable breakfast room.

Tess sat down and her shoulders slumped. 'No. I've talked to three more of Marie's so-called friends and they all say the same: yes, she was going out with a guy who was married, and no, they haven't a clue who he was.'

'Do you believe them?' asked Alec.

'I believe Sharon, because she's an emotional mess since Marie vanished and would tell anything she knew to try and help us find her, but I'm not sure about Kathy. She seemed on edge.'

'Is that Kathy Robinson?'

'Yep, do you know her?'

Alec nodded. 'I went out with her sister for a few weeks. *She* wouldn't know the truth if it hit her in the face.'

Despite feeling low Tess couldn't help but laugh. 'I think Kathy knows the truth. She just doesn't want to tell me it.'

'Why not, I wonder,' mused Alec.

'Probably because she thinks that when Marie comes back she'll go mad if her secret's been let out.'

Alec nodded. 'Could be, only why would Marie tell Kathy if she didn't tell anyone else?'

Tess frowned. 'I've tried to work that out, and the only answer I can come up with is that she *had* to tell someone. What's the point in doing something daring, something she probably thought of as sophisticated and clever, if no one can admire you for it? And let's face it, Kathy's pretty sophisticated herself. Marie would have loved to show off to her.'

'I thought Marie was popular,' said Alec, after a moment's thought. 'The things we're learning now don't tie in with that at all.'

'She was popular with you boys,' said Tess, 'but the more I talk to the girls the less I think they really liked her. Obviously the boys liked her because she was so pretty and lively. Also, she was fun to be with. You said yourself she was worth waiting for. Parties were never boring if Marie was there.'

'But?' asked Alec.

'But what?'

'You sound as though there's a downside to this.'

'Of course there is. If her girlfriends weren't really friends, if they resented her—like Annie, say—or just envied her, then maybe they're not bothered that she's vanished. Perhaps they *have* got information that would help but

103

don't see why they should give it. There could be some of them who hope she has gone to London and doesn't come back, because they're better off without her. The boys will look at them for a change.'

Alec shrugged. 'Even if you're right, how can we make them talk?'

'I don't know,' admitted Tess. 'I'm not getting anywhere so far. I even asked Richard, the guy who owns the new cinema, if he ever saw Marie there with anyone. He said he was far too busy to notice every single person who came through and told me he'd already spoken to the police and told them the same thing. He added that he thought I should leave the enquiries to the police and get on with my studies, patronizing pain!'

'Richard Young,' mused Alec thoughtfully. 'You don't think . . .'

For the second time that evening Tess was surprised to find herself laughing. 'No, I don't! He's middle-aged, going bald and has a very forceful wife who works at the cinema with him every evening. Even if she'd wanted a fling with him I can't see how Marie would have had the opportunity.'

'True, and he doesn't look the kind of man to hand out diamond watches to his lady friends,' agreed Alec with a smile, but then the smile faded and his eyes became thoughtful. 'Hey! Let me think about that for a minute. Diamond watches ring a bell. Someone I know was talking about having bought one for a song off a guy in town who'd got a job lot, probably off the back of a lorry, but I can't think who it was.' He slapped his hand against the table in frustration.

'Don't try and force it,' advised Tess. 'Let your mind turn it over subconsciously and it will come to you, probably just as you're about to fall asleep at night. That's what happens to me.'

Alec looked across the table at her. 'You're a very sensible girl, Tess. I hope Ian appreciates you.'

She felt her face go hot. 'I'm sure he does, but I'm not always sensible. I can be a bit scatterbrained sometimes.'

'What are you planning to do when

Ian takes his year out in Europe?' enquired Alec.

'As long as my GCSEs are good enough I'm going to college to do a course in childcare in September. Once I've completed that I'll either go into nursery nursing or else try and train to be a proper children's nurse, somewhere like Great Ormond Street in London, but that's not easy. There are a lot of girls after places there.'

Alec looked at her with interest. 'You and Marie aren't at all alike, are you?' he said. 'Not in looks or personality.'

'No, but neither are our parents. Marie takes after our mother while I'm like Dad. I'm the one who's good at sport and I'm built more like him too, worse luck! Marie's just like Mum, who's still attractive now and pencil-slim.'

'There's nothing wrong with curves,' he assured her, and once more Tess felt herself becoming hot. She hadn't expected compliments from Alec of all people.

'What do you think's happened to

Marie?' she asked him softly. 'Am I stupid thinking she's going to come home safely?'

Her hands were resting on the table top and Alec gently placed one of his over them. 'Not stupid, Tess, but rather optimistic. You have to face it— Marie's been missing for over two weeks now and no one has come forward to say they've seen her or spoken to her from the moment she stepped out of the Skylark Motel. If she was safe, even if she'd simply taken off like the police suggest, she wouldn't have become invisible. Not many people catch the last late-night train to King's Cross from here, but she wasn't spotted at the station that night, and neither has she rung home once to tell you not to worry. Perhaps she isn't like we all imagined, but I still believe that if she was all right she'd have contacted you or your parents.'

Tess didn't want to believe him. 'She might be in so much trouble that she doesn't dare contact us,' she said eagerly. 'She could be deliberately hiding away, hoping that everything will come right again soon.'

Alec shook his head. 'What is there to come right? No one's told us that anything was wrong in her life.'

'But there's this mystery guy, the one she was so keen on. Perhaps it's got something to do with him.'

'Such as what?' asked Alec.

Tess hung her head. 'I don't know,' she admitted. 'It's only that I can't bear to think she might never, you know, come home. That she could be . . .' She stopped, unable to say the word.

'I don't blame you for keeping hoping,' Alec assured her. 'Logically though, an outsider would have to say that the chances are you won't see her again. That could be because something's happened to her, or it could be because that's the way she wants it.'

'So, where do we go from here?' asked Tess quietly, aware that Alec's hand was still resting on hers, warm and comforting.

'I'm going to try and remember who it was who knew about those watches—hopefully that might lead somewhere. I suppose you could try Kathy Robinson again, in case you're right and she is hiding something.'

'I'll try, but she wasn't very friendly. Thank heavens Ian's working at the motel!' said Tess. 'Out of all of us he's the one in the best position to learn things. She made her phone call to me from the Skylark and she vanished the moment she stepped through their doors and out into the night—that has to mean something.'

'It might not be the motel,' said Alec, as Tess stood up and collected her shoulder bag. 'It might be the people who use it. After all, a lot of men in this town dine there or drop in for an evening drink. She could have met up with her mystery man there and vanished with him.'

'But she left alone,' protested Tess.

Alec touched her gently on the cheek. 'Sure, she left alone, but who's to say someone wasn't waiting round the corner for her?'

'We know *you* were,' Tess blurted out. As Alec stared at her, she went hot and quickly changed the subject. 'She'd phoned to say she'd be waiting up for me. She wouldn't have done that if she'd intended to be late.'

'We were only going for a quick drink,' said Alec, his expression unfathomable. 'The arrangement could have been made later, after her call. Let's face it, married men don't get many opportunities to meet their girlfriends.'

'If only we knew who he was!' said Tess as she left.

'We'll find out in the end,' promised Alec.

Tess smiled at him. 'Thanks for the evening; it's really helped. I needed to talk things over and you were the perfect listener.'

'Good. Then we must do it again some time.'

'Sure,' agreed Tess, and then remembering Ian she quickly added, 'I'll get Ian to arrange something.'

'See you then,' called Alec and Tess realized that despite her disquiet about his lack of alibi she was looking forward to their next meeting.

The next morning Tess decided to go and see Kathy Robinson again. She was sitting having breakfast, listening to the local radio and planning what to say, when suddenly she heard Kathy's name mentioned on a news flash. Startled, she stopped eating, spoon in mid-air, and listened in amazement.

Kathy Robinson is the second teenage girl to vanish in Stamfield in the last three weeks, the newscaster was continuing. *This morning, the missing girl's distraught parents told reporters of a town gripped by fear. The first girl, Marie Phillips, vanished after leaving her job as a temporary waitress at her local motel. Kathy vanished after going shopping alone late yesterday afternoon. In addition to this, a dead man was discovered in the fens on the outskirts of Stamfield around the time of Marie Phillips' disappearance, and police say that they are treating his death as suspicious. We'll bring you further news as soon as we receive more details. For now, back to the music.*

Tess's hand was shaking so much that she had to put her spoon down and she sat staring into space, unable to make any sense of what she'd heard. Before she even had time to tell her mother there was a ring at the front door, and she heard the by now familiar voice of the police sergeant who was in charge of Marie's case.

Her mother came through, her face pale. 'Tess, could you come into the front room for a moment? The police want to talk to you.'

When Tess had sat down, the WPC gave her a sympathetic smile. 'This must be very difficult for you,' she said gently.

'It's difficult for us all,' said Tess's mother.

'Of course, but according to Kathy's mother, Tess called on Kathy two days ago. Is that right, Tess?' Tess nodded silently. 'And what did you talk about?'

'Marie,' said Tess.

'What did she say about Marie?'

Tess sighed. 'Not much really, but I thought . . .'

'Yes?' asked the sergeant.

'Well, I had this feeling that she knew something but was keeping it back from me.'

'But you've no idea what it was?' asked the WPC

'No, because she kept it back from me! It was her manner; she was on edge, uncomfortable, and that isn't like her. We've known each other for years through Marie.'

'So what are you suggesting?' asked the sergeant.

'Nothing!' exclaimed Tess. 'I'm just telling you the truth.'

'The truth as you saw it,' the WPC pointed out.

'Yes, but don't you think I'm probably right? After all, Kathy's vanished now. That can't be a coincidence. What's happening in this town?'

'We don't know that anything's happening,' said the sergeant reassuringly. 'Perhaps this is something Marie and Kathy cooked up together before Marie vanished? Maybe Kathy's gone to join her in some big city and that's why she was uncomfortable talking to you.'

'But why would they do that? Marie had her boyfriend here—she wouldn't have left him.'

'You mean Alec?' asked the WPC.

'No, not Alec—the other man. The one who was married,' said Tess, desperate to get them to take this seriously.

'Well, so far he's proving a very elusive person to pin down,' said the sergeant. 'You'll appreciate that our inquiries are difficult, but we are still searching for him.'

'What about the dead man?' asked Tess's mother suddenly. 'Don't you think it's possible Marie and Kathy might have known him, and that their disappearance and his death are linked?'

'No,' said the sergeant abruptly. 'We can't find any connection at all. He was murdered and his body disposed of here. We can't be sure he'd even visited Stamfield. He might well have been dumped here to confuse us. No, your daughter and Kathy Robinson can't have known the dead man, but until we find out what's happened to them I do think that young women in the town should take extra care. We'll be putting a message out on the local TV news tonight. You know, guidelines about not walking in unlit areas alone, that sort of thing.'

'When are you going to find them?' asked Tess, her voice rising with fear. 'If you don't hurry you might be too late. How many other girls have got to go missing before you take this seriously?'

'Believe me, we're taking it very seriously indeed,' the sergeant assured her, his eyes penetrating. 'If we can only get full co-operation from both the girls' friends then I believe we'll get on a lot quicker and they'll soon be safely home with their families again.'

Tess's mother showed him and the WPC out and then returned to the front room. She and Tess stared at each other. 'He isn't so sure she's run off now, is he?' asked Tess.

Her mother's face crumpled. 'I don't know what he thinks. All I know is that I want Marie back home.' She hurried from the room, leaving Tess alone with her thoughts.

*   *   *

'What do you mean, you're taking this Karen to the pictures?' stormed Tess the following afternoon.

'How do you know she's got anything to tell you?'

'I can't be sure, but I have a feeling she knows more than she's letting on, and if I can only get her away from the motel then I've more chance of speaking freely.'

'You wouldn't bother if she wasn't pretty,' said Tess, her voice tight with anger.

Ian put his arm round her but she pushed him away and he ended up sitting on the opposite end of the park bench talking to her. 'Karen's engaged; it isn't a romantic date. We're going because we've both got the same hours off and she wants to see the Tom Cruise movie.'

'Then let her fiancé take her. How can you talk at a movie anyway?'

'We can't, but we can talk afterwards.'

'Where? In your room?' asked Tess sharply.

'No, at the pub. Come on, Tess! You're the one who wants us to do absolutely everything we can to find out the truth about Marie's disappearance. What's the matter? Don't you trust me?'

'I don't know what I feel any more, especially now Kathy's vanished,' said Tess miserably, remembering the strange tingle of excitement that she'd felt when Alec had stroked her cheek.

'Look, if this wasn't part of the investigation I wouldn't have told you about it,' said Ian reasonably. 'I didn't have to, but I did because I thought you'd be pleased.'

'I'd have thought you should be trying to talk to Eve, the receptionist who left. Why's Karen back on the scene? Or there's this Elaine you've told me about—take her out.'

'She never met Marie and she's both pretty and unattached. I thought a girl like Karen was a safer bet. Honestly,

Tess, this isn't like you. Have I ever played around since we became an item?'

'No,' she admitted.

'Then why should I start now?'

'Because you'll soon be leaving anyway so it doesn't matter any more,' she said reluctantly.

Ian moved up the bench to sit closer to her again, and this time she didn't push him away. 'Tess, we've always known I was going away. We've had a good time, and it isn't over yet, but you've got plans for your future and I've got plans for mine.'

'The trouble is,' admitted Tess, 'that with Marie vanishing the way she has I'm scared of losing anyone else. We used to talk together so much. Even when we argued we always made up and we used to have loads of laughs. Now I haven't got anyone to talk to except you and Alec. It's terrible at home—you can't imagine what the parents are like.'

'What about Liz and Patsy? They're your closest friends. Wouldn't it help to talk it over with them?'

'Liz is working for her dad. She's the office dogsbody but at least it's a job and she's getting money.'

'Well, Patsy then?' persisted Ian.

'Patsy's been in Italy. She only got back yesterday.'

'Why not call in on her this evening? At least it will get you out of the house, and you two always gossip for hours!'

'Well, if you're going to the pictures with Karen tonight then I might as well,' said Tess.

Ian gave her a hug. 'That's more like the Tess I know. Tell you what, I'll call you when I get in tonight and tell you everything I learn from Karen.'

Tess had to be content with that, but she found it difficult to enjoy the short time she had with Ian before he went off to do the midday shift at the motel.

*   *   *

During the evening meal Tess was still feeling miserable and despite her own grief and anxiety her mother noticed.

'Is something wrong, Tess?' she asked.

119

'Only the usual,' mumbled Tess, unwilling to inflict her personal problems on her mother at this time.

'Things all right with you and Ian?' persisted her mother.

'Yes, fine,' said Tess shortly. 'Not that it matters. He's off to Europe as soon as I go back to college so I won't be seeing him after that.'

'He will be coming back,' her mother pointed out.

'Sure, but he won't be the same, will he? I mean, that's the whole point of a year out. You're meant to grow up, change, gain life experience. What's the point in going if you're going to come back the same person? I think it's stupid anyway. Everyone gets life experience right up until they're dead.'

As soon as the words were out she realized what she'd said and her eyes widened as she stared at her mother in horror. 'I'm sorry, Mum. I didn't mean . . .'

Her mother smiled over-brightly. 'Don't be silly, Tess. You can't watch every word because Marie's missing. We all have to go on living some kind of life while we wait.'

'I'm going to call round and see Patsy tonight,' said Tess in a rush, anxious to divert her mother.

'Good idea. You haven't been able to see her much this holiday, have you? But I think your father should take you. I saw the early evening news tonight, and like the sergeant said, they advised all young girls to be very careful.'

*   *   *

Patsy lived in a pretty terraced house in the road opposite the park. Tess climbed out of her father's car and walked into the tiny square of front garden to ring the bell. Her father didn't drive off until he saw Patsy's mother open the front door.

'Tess! How lovely to see you!' she exclaimed with a smile, but then she remembered about Marie and the smile faded. 'We were so sorry to hear about your sister,' she added in the low voice that Tess found people often used now when talking about Marie.

121

'We only got home yesterday morning, but our neighbours told us straight away. It was a terrible shock. How are your poor parents coping?'

'They're doing the best they can,' said Tess, wishing Patsy would arrive and put an end to the conversation. She hated this kind of talk because she never knew what to say. How did people imagine they were coping? She always wanted to say that it was ghastly, like a nightmare, only none of them could wake up, but her natural manners stopped her. People meant well, they just didn't know what to say.

At that moment Patsy came running down the stairs, heated rollers in her hair. 'Tess! Why didn't you ring and say you were coming? Now you've caught me at my worst! Come on up, we can have a good chat in the bedroom. What do you think of my tan?'

'Fantastic,' said Tess honestly. She'd never seen Patsy look so well.

Once in her bedroom, Patsy's smile faded. 'I'm so sorry about Marie,' she said, taking hold of Tess's hand. 'I wanted to ring straight away, but Mum

122

wouldn't let me. She said your parents probably wanted the line kept free in case you got any news.'

'Yes, every time the phone rings we do jump,' admitted Tess. 'It's just so awful I can't explain. It's as though life's stopped, and you're just marking time until Marie comes home again. The police aren't that helpful either. Well, I don't think they are.

'You see, Marie had this secret boyfriend, a married man. She used to tell me about him although she never mentioned his name. She was dead keen on him, and I know she wouldn't have run off to London and left him, but because no one knows his name, and she was so secretive about him only a few of us know about him, and no one ever saw him. If only we knew who he was I'm sure the police would stop thinking Marie had run off and pursue other lines of enquiry, but no matter how hard I try I can't come up with a name for him.

'Marie was so secretive, and since she vanished I've learned that she wasn't always that nice to people, which probably doesn't help either. But I miss her, Patsy. Of course she had faults, we all do, but she's my sister and I love her. Home isn't the same without her. I want her back, but I don't know what else I can do to make the police take me seriously. The only person they seem to suspect might have had anything to do with her disappearance, if she hasn't run off, is Alec.'

'Alec? That gorgeous boy who works at the garage?' asked Patsy.

'Yes.'

'Well, she did see him, didn't she?'

'Yes, they went out sometimes, but it was the married man she was serious about.'

'Could they have rowed, do you think?' Patsy asked.

'Yes, they could have done!' exploded Tess. 'That's the trouble—there's lots of things that *could* have happened but nothing we can be sure of. Alec was meant to meet her the night she vanished, but he says she stood him up and he went for a drive on his motorbike instead.'

'So, no alibi?' asked Patsy.

'That's right, no alibi. But no motive either.'

'Jealousy?'

Tess shook her head. 'I don't think he's the type. Anyway, Patsy, if Alec did do something to Marie, what's happened to her body? And how come Kathy Robinson's disappeared too?'

'Well, do you think this married man was involved with Kathy as well then?' asked Patsy.

Tess shook her head. 'No! Yes! I haven't a clue. How can I know anything when I've no idea who he is?'

'Look,' said Patsy gently, 'I didn't know about any of this. I mean, we only got back yesterday, but I feel really guilty now that I didn't get in touch with you right away once I did hear.'

'Why? What could you have done?' asked Tess dispiritedly.

'I could have told you who Marie's married man was.'

Tess's head shot up and she stared at her friend in amazement. 'You what?'

'I know who Marie was seeing secretly. I saw her with the man in Nottingham just before we went off to

125

Italy. I was in a nightclub with Gary, so I'd really rather you didn't mention this to Mum. She'd probably try and stop me seeing him and I couldn't bear that.'

'I won't tell anyone where I got his name from,' promised Tess, her heart thumping against her ribs. 'Come on, Patsy, this could be vitally important. Who was the man you saw Marie with?'

'Mark Kingsley,' said Patsy softly. 'The owner of our new nightclub, Take Four.'

CHAPTER SEVEN

'Mark Kingsley?' exclaimed Alec in amazement. 'But he's got two young children, and a stunning wife.'

'I know,' said Tess sadly. 'I couldn't believe it either, but Patsy was adamant that's who it was. You didn't mind me coming round here, did you? I couldn't think of anyone else I could talk it over with.'

'I'm delighted you came,' said Alec, giving her a warm smile. 'I only wish you'd brought different news.'

'It explains why Marie was so anxious to keep the affair quiet,' reasoned Tess. 'She'd have been very unpopular in the town if anyone had found out.'

'It explains something else as well,' said Alec.

'What?' asked Tess.

'The watch you mentioned. I remember now that it was when I was in Take Four the other night that I was told Mark had some good watches for sale at a very reasonable price if I was interested. He's meant to have some relation in the trade, but whether that's true or not I don't know. It's more likely they fell off the back of the proverbial lorry.'

Tess fidgeted in her chair. 'Alec, how well do you know Mark Kingsley?'

'Hardly at all. I've spoken to him a couple of times at the club and his car's been in for a service once, but that's all. Why?'

'I just wondered if you thought he

was the kind of person who could be violent,' said Tess anxiously.

Alec thought for a moment. 'Yeah, I guess he could. He has to be tough at the nightclub—you know what it's like at one in the morning when everyone's had too much to drink. He's a big guy too. He works out at Pete's Gym—I've seen him there. If someone annoyed him enough he might turn nasty.'

It wasn't the answer Tess had wanted to hear. 'Do you think Marie might have annoyed him?' she asked quietly.

'She could have done.'

Tess bit her bottom lip. 'Do you think he might have killed her?'

Her voice shook and without thinking Alec moved to sit on the arm of her chair and put both his arms round her in a comforting embrace. 'Tess, don't torment yourself like this. Anything's possible, but at the moment we don't know anything for certain. I can't bear seeing you so uptight all the time.'

'It's the not knowing,' said Tess, her voice muffled by his thick denim shirt. 'Even if she's dead I'd rather know.

128

Can you understand that?'

Alec stroked her brown curly hair in a gentle rhythmic movement. 'Sure I can. But as we don't know we're doing the next best thing, trying to find out the truth, and thanks to you we've taken a big step forward today.'

For a moment Tess enjoyed the sensation of leaning against him and the tangy scent of his aftershave, but then she remembered Ian and quickly drew away. 'But what happens now?' she went on. 'We can hardly march up to Mark Kingsley and say "Did you murder Marie Phillips because she was endangering your marriage?" '

'No, but I can get some of my friends to start asking questions, find out if anyone they know ever saw him with Marie, and if so what the relationship looked like. Let's say they were often seen quarrelling or something, that would give us a clue. At least then we'd know that it wasn't all jewellery and sweet romance.'

'What about the police?'

'What about them?' demanded Alec, his face darkening. 'They haven't been very helpful so far; in fact, I seem to have been their main suspect. Only this morning they were still trying to check my alibi for the night Marie disappeared by stopping cars on the top road where I went for a spin and talking to the drivers.'

'It drives me mad,' said Tess heatedly. 'They won't listen to us, the people who knew her best. They have to go off and make their own decisions, based on nothing at all.'

'Except the fact that I'd arranged to meet her and don't have an alibi,' said Alec dryly.

Tess felt uncomfortable. 'It's a pity no one saw you anywhere that night,' she said.

He grinned at her. 'Yeah, it is. Would you like to pretend you did?'

Tess went hot all over, and she felt very awkward. 'I can't, Alec! I was at the barbecue, and anyway I couldn't lie to them. You know you're innocent, so there's nothing to worry about. I'm sorry, but ...'

Alec raised an eyebrow. 'It was a joke, Tess! You were the one who was worried. As you say, I know I've nothing to hide. The thing that's worrying me is, do *you* believe that?'

Tess couldn't meet his eyes. 'Yes, of course I do,' she said vehemently, but she wasn't sure Alec believed her and all at once she wished they weren't alone together.

'Did it make you jealous?' asked Tess curiously.

Alec sensed her unease. 'Marie wasn't that important to me, Tess. I fancied her and we had some good evenings, but while I was waiting there were plenty of other girls I liked nearly as much.'

'Lucky them!' said Tess sarcastically, failing to notice the pain in Alec's eyes. 'I hope they didn't realize they were just filling in the time for you until my sister became completely free.'

'They were casual relationships, nothing heavy,' said Alec gently. 'No one was misled or hurt, Tess. It wasn't like you and Ian, who've been an item for ages now.'

'Yes, well, I hope we still are after he finishes spending the evening with

131

Karen,' said Tess, turning a little pink as she realized that they would just about be leaving the cinema.

'It's all being done for Marie,' Alec reminded her.

'I know. Everything's done for Marie these days.'

'Not quite everything,' said Alec. 'When I put my arms round you, I did it for us—for you and me. Marie didn't come into my mind at all.'

Their eyes met and Tess's stomach did a funny dip. 'It's time I went,' she said quickly. 'Ian's going to ring me when he gets back and fill me in on what's gone on.'

'Sure,' agreed Alec equably. 'Look, I'm not working Sunday. Why don't the three of us take a few sandwiches and some drinks to Ropsley Woods and have lunch there while we try and put the information we've got into some kind of order? I can borrow my dad's car—he won't mind.'

'Sounds a good idea,' agreed Tess. 'I'll check it out with Ian and then he can let you know. Thanks for listening.'

She gave him a brief smile and at the

door he rested a hand lightly on her shoulder. 'See you Sunday then.'

As Tess left they both knew that somehow, in a very small way, their relationship had just changed, and her earlier fear was forgotten.

*   *   *

Ian and Karen took a seat in a quiet corner of the Blue Boar pub, and over drinks discussed the movie for a time.

'It was a bit violent for my liking,' said Karen.

'It's a violent world these days, as that Marie girl from the motel has almost certainly found out to her cost.'

Karen's face changed. 'Yes, well, like I said I'm sorry if anything's happened to her, but she wasn't exactly sensitive, you know.'

'Wasn't she?'

Karen gave a sarcastic laugh. 'She pretended to be. When the boss was around she was all sweetness and light, but she didn't give a toss what the other girls thought of her.'

'You mean, she wasn't friendly with

the other girls?' asked Ian.

'No way! She liked older men, we all knew that. I mean, there was one guy she was dating, or so I was told, and apparently he used to come to the motel for a meal sometimes and then wait until her shift ended and walk her home. He was years older than her, and he wore a wedding ring. Well, whatever turns you on! I mean, I quite like older guys myself—my fiancé's five years older than me—but she fancied Keith Palmer as well and made that very clear.'

'Did anyone tell the police this?' asked Ian.

Karen shrugged. 'I didn't, because it was just gossip to me. I never saw this man. Someone else might have done.'

Aware that Karen was probably a mine of useful information if he could only keep her talking, Ian tried not to seem too obsessed in case she got suspicious as to why he was interested. He excused himself, bought them both another drink, and then smiled at her. 'Surely you were prettier than this Marie girl, weren't you?'

Karen smiled back. 'Nice of you to say so, but you never met her, did you? No, when Marie got herself done up she was a knockout. She had these incredible never-ending legs which were always on display. She was special, we could see that, but it didn't make her any more popular.'

'I don't suppose it did. Keith Palmer seems pretty friendly towards everyone though; was Marie treated differently from the rest of you?'

'Wasn't she just! By the time she left, well, vanished I suppose I should say, she could twist him round her little finger. She was allowed to change her shifts when they didn't suit her, and no one's meant to do that unless there's illness in the family. Then he let her smoke in between breaks outside the kitchen door, which annoyed the other smokers who had to wait, and he sometimes gave her a lift home after work.'

'Did you girls tell the police all this?' asked Ian, with interest.

Karen shook her head. 'Not likely! We'd have sounded like a catty jealous crowd who disliked her for being good-looking, but it wasn't that, it really wasn't. Marie just wasn't a nice girl.'

'I take it Keith Palmer isn't married,' queried Ian, inwardly reeling from all he was learning.

'No, he's divorced. He's got a girlfriend though—more than a girlfriend, I suppose. I mean, they live together in a flat over the motel garages.'

'Good job she didn't find out,' said Ian with feeling.

Karen glanced sideways at him, hesitated and then leant forward. 'To be honest, Ian, some of us think she did. She used to help around the place, you know, provide an extra pair of hands on special occasions like wedding receptions. I remember once Marie came into the rest room laughing because Petra, that's the girlfriend, had caught her and Keith together in the wine cellar. They were just collecting some bottles according to Marie, but Petra flipped. I'm sure Marie was lying anyway—the waitresses never fetch the wine.'

'This married man she used to date, the one who came to the motel and waited to take her home, was he there the night she vanished?' asked Ian.

'Couldn't say. No one's mentioned it. You know, you're very interested in Marie, aren't you? Why?'

Ian thought quickly. 'I'm thinking about going into the police force after my year out,' he bluffed. 'A mystery like this fascinates me. I mean, Marie must be somewhere. No one just vanishes, except in sci-fi movies.'

Karen nodded. 'Yeah, she's somewhere all right, but I bet you any money you like she's dead.'

'Why do you say that? The police are sure she's run off to London.'

'I'm sure because on the day she disappeared she was full of herself, bursting with some great piece of news that she'd learnt. I heard her talking about it to someone on the motel telephone, the one we're not supposed to use.'

'Did anyone else hear her talking then?'

Karen thought hard. 'Not likely,

really. It's a quiet corridor and I just happened to brush past her but I caught a few words.'

'Did you ask her what it was about?' enquired Ian.

Karen smiled. 'Of course I did; I'm as inquisitive as the next person, but she wouldn't say. She went into her Madam Mystery role and I didn't push her because I didn't want her to know how much she was annoying me!'

'I must say, she doesn't sound the nicest of people,' said Ian, glad that he hadn't brought Tess along to hear these revelations about her sister.

'No, she wasn't, but she still didn't deserve to die,' said Karen firmly.

'We don't know she *is* dead,' Ian reminded her.

'Well, if she isn't, why hasn't anyone heard from her?' asked Karen. 'And what about the dead man found in the fens? I think there's a murderer loose in this town and he's probably killed the second girl, Kathy, too. I don't go anywhere on my own now.'

Ian had no answer to this, and knew that if he was honest he agreed with

Karen. Marie was probably dead, but it was still up to him, Tess and Alec to find out how she'd died and who was responsible for her murder.

'I enjoyed this evening,' said Karen brightly. 'We must do it again.'

'Sure,' said Ian automatically, and then shivered as he realized that it was almost certain Marie would never see another film again.

CHAPTER EIGHT

Luckily Ian was free on Sunday as well, and so he and Tess were able to join Alec for lunch in Ropsley Woods. The weather had turned very hot and the ground was cracking badly as Tess picked her way carefully over the bare earth of the once green parking area and through into the trees where they intended to eat.

Because Ian had worked until late on Saturday, Tess had only had a brief phone conversation with him since the night he and Karen had gone out. She was looking forward to hearing the details and to the three of them discussing it all.

'How are your parents?' Alec asked her when they were settled.

'Dad's gone to London to show Marie's photo around and see if anyone can remember seeing her. He's like I am, better if he's doing something. Mum's the opposite: she's tired all the time and can hardly find the energy to do everyday things.'

'Right,' said Ian briskly, getting out a notepad and pencil. 'Let's get down to facts. What exactly do we now know about Marie's life leading up to the night she vanished?'

'We know she'd been dating Mark Kingsley,' said Tess, ticking the points off on her fingers. 'And we know too that he gave her some nice presents: clothes, jewellery, perfume . . .'

'Perfume?'

At Alec's interruption, Tess turned to him. 'Did I forget to mention that? I found a huge bottle of Chanel No. 5 hidden in her dressing table drawer. She'd never have bought that for herself; Mark must have chosen it.'

'Perhaps he's got a friend in the perfume trade as well,' said Alec, but he seemed to be paying more attention to the discovery than Tess thought necessary.

'Do we know where they used to go? Or what their relationship was like?' asked Ian.

'I've put the word about—you know, asking all my mates for information,' said Alec. 'So far I haven't got much back, but one mate rang me this morning to say that a friend of his saw the pair of them in a pub in Nottingham and that they were definitely arguing. At least, Marie was arguing. My mate was told that Mark Kingsley was trying to quieten her down all the time.'

'When was that?' asked Tess.

'About six weeks before she vanished.'

'It doesn't mean much,' pointed out Ian. 'Everyone has rows. Tess and I certainly do, but she's still here!' he laughed.

Tess stared at him. 'I don't think

that's very funny, Ian,' she said indignantly.

'Sorry, black humour. I get this creepy feeling when we're talking about Marie. It was a tasteless attempt to make myself feel better.'

'What doesn't make sense to me,' said Alec, 'is why Mark Kingsley would want to harm Marie.'

'That's obvious,' said Ian. 'She wanted him to leave his wife and he had no intention of doing any such thing.'

'But Marie wouldn't have wanted him to leave, would she?' Alec persisted. 'Let's think about it logically. Marie hated Stamfield—she was bored to death here. Why would she want to get tied down to a guy who'd just moved into the area and clearly had plans to stick around for some time while he made as much money as he could? Marie was ambitious; she wanted more from life than that.'

They were quiet for a few minutes. 'That's true,' admitted Tess. 'On the other hand, maybe it was a power thing. You know, she didn't want him permanently but she wanted to show that she could have him if she liked.'

'Do you believe Marie's mind worked that way?' asked Alec.

'No. OK, I admit that from what we hear Marie wasn't quite the person I thought, but she wasn't small-minded like that. She'd never have wanted to split up a family just to show that she could.'

'I agree,' said Alec, 'which, in my opinion, lets Mark Kingsley off the hook as the chief suspect.'

'I think you're wrong,' said Ian. 'He was always going to the Skylark to eat and then he'd hang around until Marie's shift ended and they'd go off together. Who else would she have gone off with willingly?'

'Well, me,' said Alec abruptly. 'I'd met her from work before.' There was an awkward silence.

'We don't know that she did go willingly,' said Tess, deciding to ignore the remark as Ian hadn't responded.

Alec took a bite out of one of the picnic rolls and stared up through the trees at the patches of blue sky. Even now, at moments like this, when he faced the fact that he would probably never see Marie again, he'd get a tight ache in his throat. She'd been so lovely, enjoyed life so much, and here they all were on a lovely summer Sunday without her. She was like a fourth invisible member of the group, haunting him in a way he'd never admit to anyone.

'Alec!' said Tess loudly.

He came back to reality with a jump. 'Sorry.'

She stared at him. 'What do you think, about her not going willingly?'

He finished his roll and looked into Tess's warm brown eyes, the complete opposite of Marie's piercing blue ones. 'I think that if she'd put up a struggle, resisted in any way, then the police would have found some clues. You know: trampled grass, a dropped button or piece of fabric. If you have a struggle there's always something for the forensic people to check out.'

'Perhaps Keith Palmer gave her a lift,' said Ian. 'Let's face it, he'd done it before and she was obviously keen on him.'

'She left on her own,' said Tess wearily. 'The receptionist was adamant about that.'

'Trouble is, you can't find the receptionist,' Alec pointed out to Ian.

Ian flushed. 'That's hardly my fault. I've done pretty well if you ask me. The turnover of staff's amazing on Reception and so far no one's given me the name of the girl who saw her go.'

'Then that's what you should concentrate on,' said Alec. 'If you can't find out maybe your parents could get the girl's name from the police, Tess.'

'I thought it might have been in the local paper at the time, but it wasn't,' said Tess. 'When I went through a copy at the library it just said *the duty receptionist reported that* ... Useless.'

Alec yawned suddenly and the other two stared at him. 'Sorry,' he said quickly. 'I'm not bored, I'm whacked. I've never known the garage so busy. Lots of cars are coming in for repair work these days, and none of it's done under insurance. The garage owner doesn't mind—cash payments suit him—but the owners are always in a hurry.'

'Whose cars are they?' asked Ian.

'Not many are local. Reps, people staying a few nights in town on business, that kind of thing. Everyone's on to tax fiddles and some of the owners look a bit dodgy, but work's work.'

They talked for a long time about what they'd learned so far and how they felt, but by the time they picked up their rubbish and went back to the car they were no further forward in working out what had happened to Marie. They had ideas, they could make guesses, but there was nothing concrete that they could go to the police with in order to persuade them to increase the amount of time they were spending on the case.

'Even if they'd found her body they probably wouldn't be able to catch the killer,' said Ian as they drove home.

'Why do you say that?' asked Alec.

'Because of this guy they found in the fens. They've plastered posters of his face all over town and in every local

146

and free paper, but no one's come forward with anything. The only way they'd catch a killer is if he or she were trapped by a video camera,' replied Ian.

Tess shivered. She didn't want to think about Marie's body, or Marie's possible killer. She wanted Marie safely home again.

Alec pulled up in the street where Tess lived, a few doors down from her house. 'Right, what are our plans for next week then?'

'I want to confront Mark Kingsley,' said Tess firmly. 'I want to see the expression in his eyes when I tell him that I know he was going out with my sister.'

'That's too dangerous, Tess,' said Ian quickly.

'I don't care; it's what I want to do. If I go to Take Four on Tuesday night he's bound to be there at eight o'clock. It's the "Happy Hour" and my friends say he keeps a close eye on everyone then.'

'That's true,' confirmed Alec. 'If you go with her, Ian, she'll be safe enough.

After all, what can he do in front of so many witnesses?'

'But I can't go with her,' explained Ian. 'I'm working again.'

'Can you take me, Alec?' asked Tess eagerly.

'Sure, if Ian doesn't mind.'

'What about your work?' asked Ian. 'I thought you said you were working late most nights.'

'I'll make sure I finish on time on Tuesday.'

Tess knew that Ian wasn't happy, but she refused to let it worry her. She hadn't been happy when he'd taken Karen out, but it hadn't stopped him. She wanted to go out with Alec for the same reason that Ian had gone out with Karen—to find out more about Marie's life when she wasn't with them.

'Thanks, Alec, you're a pal!' she exclaimed, scrambling from the car. 'Ian, are you coming in for a bit?'

He shook his head. 'I think I'll get on home. Stuff to do and that—you know how it is.'

Tess looked back into the car with a strange cold feeling gripping her stomach.

'Are we going out this evening?' They always went out on Sunday nights so the question wasn't unreasonable but Ian looked uncomfortable.

'Sorry, Tess, I can't. I'm really whacked with working all these odd hours at the Skylark, and to make it worse I'm sleeping badly. I'll give you a ring in the next day or two, fix something up for later in the week.'

Tess felt her face flush and she looked at Alec, but he was staring impassively through the windscreen.

'Well,' she said awkwardly, 'if you really haven't the energy to come out I suppose that's it. I hope you don't tire this easily when you're trekking round the world in the autumn.'

Before Ian could reply she slammed the passenger door behind her. She knew it was a rotten thing to say but he'd behaved in a really odd way and she felt bewildered and confused.

'What was all that about?' asked Alec as they drove off.

'Like I said, I'm tired,' said Ian shortly. Alec didn't say any more.

At ten past eight on the following Tuesday evening Tess and Alec walked into the Take Four nightclub and looked around the crowded room.

'Is he here?' asked Tess, raising her voice in order to be heard over the noise of the disco.

Alec glanced about. 'Doesn't look like it, but don't worry—he'll be along. I've never been here on a Tuesday and not seen him.'

Tess felt a bit unsure of herself. She and her friends didn't hang out here very much; she'd only been once before, and that was with Ian when it had just opened. Finding herself here with Alec, who as usual looked devastatingly handsome in his smart casuals, made her awkward. She felt that her long black skirt and silver blouse with a multi-coloured waistcoat she'd found in the Red Cross charity shop, wasn't quite the right outfit, but when they sat down at a corner table and Alec brought her some Diet Coke he quickly got rid of her worries.

'Great outfit! Love the waistcoat. Do you want to dance?'

She hesitated, wondering briefly if she ought to dance with Alec, especially since she was starting to feel undeniable flickerings of attraction towards him, but then she remembered the way Ian had dismissed her on Sunday and decided there was nothing to stop her.

'Love to. I should warn you that I'm out of practice. Ian doesn't like dancing.'

'You'll soon get back into it; I remember seeing you dance at Marie's eighteenth party—you were really good.'

He was right, Tess was a good dancer and she was very soon lost in the beat of the music. When her body brushed against Alec's on the crowded square of floor set aside for dancing she felt a tingle of excitement. He grinned at her. 'See? I told you! You should dance more.'

In between dancing they drank Cokes and chatted and the time flew by. When Alec leant across the table to tap Tess on the arm and attract her attention she was startled to see from her watch that it was already nine-fifteen.

'What is it?' she asked.

He moved his head slightly to his right. 'Look over there. Mark Kingsley's standing by the bar.'

Tess examined the owner of the nightclub carefully. She knew immediately that Patsy had been telling the truth. This was exactly the kind of older man Marie would have found attractive. He was tall and well built with a shock of dark brown hair and brown eyes that shone with intelligence. He was well dressed too, in a dark suit, pale blue shirt and blue and gold tie, although he wore too much jewellery for Tess's liking.

'What do you want to do now?' queried Alec.

'Speak to him, of course,' said Tess, getting to her feet.

'Hey, hang about! You can't just march up to him and blurt out something about Marie.'

'You watch me!' said Tess, and she set off across the floor, pushing the dancers aside with ruthless determination. Alec quickly followed her. He knew Mark Kingsley had a reputation for possessing a fiery temper and wanted to be there when Tess spoke.

Mark Kingsley was with two friends, both of whom were laughing loudly at some joke he'd made as Tess walked up to them. She planted herself squarely in front of him and stared straight into his eyes. The laughter died away but Mark Kingsley looked at her with some amusement.

'Are you old enough to be in this club, little girl?' he asked lazily.

Tess ignored his friends' laughter. 'Yes. I'm here for a special reason,' she added.

'Let me guess ... it's your tenth birthday!' he retorted and again his friends roared with laughter, but Tess remained stony faced.

'Actually, I'm here to look for my sister.'

'Really?' Kingsley glanced round the

packed club. 'Good luck then. There must be over seventy people here tonight.'

'Is my sister one of them?' asked Tess, her legs feeling wobbly despite her steady voice.

'Now, how would I know?' he asked, clearly becoming bored with her, although he'd noticed Alec coming up behind her and acknowledged him with a brief nod of the head.

'Because you're a good friend of hers, or at least, you used to be.'

'I'm a very good friend to lots of girls. What's your sister's name?'

'Marie Phillips,' said Tess loudly.

Both she and Alec saw the blood drain from Mark Kingsley's face, and his two friends vanished with startling speed, leaving him quite alone at the bar.

He stared at Tess in disbelief. 'You're Marie Phillips' sister?'

'Yes.'

'But you don't look anything like her.'

'Lucky for me,' said Tess. 'At least it means I'm still around.'

'Look, I'm really sorry that your sister's gone missing, but it's nothing to do with me. Get real! Masses of girls come to this place five nights a week. What they do in their private life isn't my responsibility. She wasn't even here the night she vanished, was she? I thought I read that she'd been working at the Skylark Motel.'

'She had,' said Tess, 'but we've been told you often used to meet her there after work and walk her home.'

Now the colour flooded back into Kingsley's face and his cheeks turned blotchy. 'I don't know what you're talking about,' he blustered.

'I think you do,' said Alec quietly. 'You and Marie were also seen on a trip to Nottingham, and you were obviously *very* good friends.'

Kingsley swallowed hard, saw that there were several people within earshot and jerked his head towards a door behind the bar.

'You'd better come through to the back. We can talk more privately there,' he muttered. With a sigh of relief Tess followed him, and as they

155

entered the small room she felt Alec give her hand an encouraging squeeze.

In his own office, away from the noisy throng of dancers, Mark Kingsley seemed to regain some of his earlier poise. He sat down behind a small desk and indicated that Alec and Tess should sit down opposite him. He wasn't smiling, but his colour was back to normal and his eyes had lost their initial fearful expression.

'It's true that I met Marie once in Nottingham,' he said carefully, 'but it was a chance meeting. She was there shopping and I often have to go on business.'

'And you got very friendly very quickly, did you?' asked Tess rudely.

Kingsley bit hard on his lower lip—a sure sign of irritation, Alec thought. 'Put like that it sounds unlikely, I know, but we both had a few drinks and that's how it happened.'

'She told me about you,' said Tess. 'She thought you were fantastic, a really great guy. She was madly in love with you.'

'If she said that, she was lying. Marie

didn't always tell the truth,' he retorted.

'How do you know that?' demanded Alec.

Kingsley's complexion became mottled once more. 'I don't know for certain, but I've heard people talking about her and that seems to be the general impression.'

'So you weren't the older man she was seeing?' challenged Tess. 'If I go to the police and tell them you were, you'll be able to prove I'm wrong, will you?'

There was silence in the room as Kingsley stared at the two young people opposite him.

'If you go to the police and tell them that,' he said at last, 'I shall not only deny it, I shall consult my solicitor about damages for slander.'

'But you used to eat at the Skylark and wait for Marie's shift to finish so that you could take her home!' cried Tess in exasperation. 'Lots of people will vouch for that.'

'If I was eating there late at night I'd give her a lift, yes. What's wrong with that? It's not a very safe walk back along by the canal.'

'What makes you think she took that route?' asked Alec quietly. 'How do you know she didn't go down to the main road and walk along there?'

'I've had enough of this,' said Kingsley impatiently. 'You come into my club and then start making unsubstantiated charges against me in full view of everyone. You're lucky I haven't thrown you out before this.'

'You could have done,' Tess pointed out.

'Well, I didn't. I felt sorry for you. The way your sister has vanished into thin air's terrible, but it has nothing to do with me. If I get to hear that you're suggesting to anyone that it does then, as I said, you'll find yourselves in serious legal trouble. Take my advice— leave this to the police.'

Tess opened her mouth to protest, to shout that he couldn't do this, not just sit there and flatly deny everything, but then Alec shot her a look and she fell silent.

'Sorry, Mark,' he said casually. 'As

you rightly say, it's a total nightmare for Tess and all Marie's family and friends. If anyone tells Tess anything, however small, she feels she has to follow it up because the police don't seem to be doing anything.'

'Sure, I can understand that,' said Kingsley, but his eyes were watchful.

Alec leant towards him. 'Look, there's something I wanted to ask you. Something that doesn't have anything to do with all this.'

'What's that then?'

Alec looked straight at Tess. 'Wait outside a moment, would you, Tess? This is private.'

She was furious, but something about Alec's expression made her do as he asked and she walked out, banging the door to behind her.

'Spirited!' said Kingsley, with a man-to-man smile.

'Yes,' agreed Alec, trying hard to conceal his dislike for the man. 'Mark, I'm going out with this woman. You know how it is—she's a bit older than me and her family are loaded but when it comes to looks . . .'

'I get the picture!' grinned Kingsley.

'Trouble is, it's her birthday next week and I don't earn enough at the garage to get her something special. Chris Forster told me that you knew someone in the jewellery trade. He said you could sometimes get things a bit cheaper. Is that true?'

'Sure!' said Kingsley, relaxing once more and basking in his own importance. 'You name it, I'll see you get a bargain. What did you have in mind?'

'A watch of some sort. I can afford a cheap one, but I want it to be a proper piece of jewellery as well. You know, something she'll wear in the evenings, when we go out.'

'No problem,' laughed Kingsley, tipping back his chair and swivelling round to open the safe behind him. 'Chris was right. And as it happens I've got some watches here right now. I've been selling them off to selected friends for a few weeks. Just remember this next time my car comes in for a service, will you?'

'I certainly will,' agreed Alec,

holding his breath in suspense.

At last Mark turned back to him and opened his right hand to reveal a small diamond-studded wrist-watch. 'What do you think of that?' he asked, proudly.

'I think,' said Alec with satisfaction, 'that it's identical to the one you gave Marie a few days before she died.'

CHAPTER NINE

For a terrible moment after he'd spoken, Alec thought that Kingsley was going to attack him. He half-rose from his seat and leant across the desk with his hands outstretched but then clearly thought better of it and slowly sank down into his chair again.

'Very clever,' he admitted slowly. 'I'd quite forgotten giving one of those watches to Marie, but you're right, of course. No doubt you've got it hidden away somewhere safely as well?'

'Naturally,' agreed Alec, sounding a great deal more calm than he felt now that he'd seen for himself the kind of temper Mark Kingsley possessed.

The nightclub owner lit a cigarette and inhaled deeply. 'OK, I admit it. Marie and I were an item, for want of a better expression. We used to get away together whenever we could, which wasn't as often as either of us would have liked what with this job and my family.'

'Must have been difficult,' agreed Alec, trying to keep any trace of sarcasm out of his voice.

'I know what you're thinking,' continued Kingsley. 'You're wondering what I was doing playing around with a teenager when I'm a married man. But you knew Marie—surely you can understand the attraction?'

'Of course. I fancied her myself, but I'm single.'

'Look, I'm not trying to say that what we did was right, but it's the way it was. I'm not the first married man to have an affair.'

'Why didn't you tell the police?'

Kingsley stared at him in astonishment. 'Are you mad? First of all my wife would have been bound to find out, and that was the last thing I wanted. Secondly, well, I do a bit of work apart from this club, work that the taxman doesn't know about. Once you bring the police into your life they poke and pry into every corner. This jewellery that I sell off, it's got nothing to do with Marie's disappearance but they'd still have made sure it got reported.'

'And you?' asked Alec quietly. 'Did you have anything to do with her disappearance?'

'No, I did not,' said Kingsley, his voice low and hard. 'I never saw her on the day she vanished. I was busy with this place. There was trouble over an order and I had to see to that. We were meant to meet up when her shift ended and I was going to walk her back to her place. We often used to do that—it was a useful chance for a quick meeting— but in the end I couldn't make it.'

'Did she ring you? Ask where you were when you didn't turn up?' asked Alec.

Kingsley shook his head. 'Marie

would never have done anything like that. She knew better than to try and contact me. I'd warned her that if my wife got wind of anything I'd drop her like a shot. No, on the days I couldn't make arranged meetings she'd hang around for about ten minutes and then go home, or so she told me.'

'Pity no one can back your story up,' said Alec casually. 'After all, Marie's the only one who can vouch for the fact that you're telling the truth, and she happens to have vanished.'

'Yes,' agreed Kingsley, rising to his feet. 'And now I'll give you a piece of advice that you'd do well to take on board. If any of our conversation gets back to the police or if my wife gets any kind of anonymous tip-off about my affair, I'll know where the information came from and I won't be happy—not at all happy.' His voice was threatening.

'Marie's family aren't happy either,' said Alec bravely.

'I had nothing to do with her disappearance!' shouted Kingsley. 'If you try to imply that I did then I shall have my solicitors on to you for slander.'

'It wouldn't be slanderous to tell the police you were the married man Marie was seeing; it would be the truth,' retorted Alec.

Kingsley's eyes narrowed. 'I've warned you, Alec. Now get out of here, and take Marie's sister with you. That family's brought me quite enough trouble already. Just leave it, if you know what's good for you, get it?'

Alec got out of his chair and looked at the night-club owner with contempt. 'Yes, I've "got it" as you say. I've got it very well. You're a cheating, lying coward who hasn't the guts to tell the police the truth because it might upset your cosy little world. What about Marie? Suppose your information could help them find her?'

'How could it?' snapped Kingsley. 'I didn't see her that day and I've no idea what happened to her. If you want my opinion, she's gone to London. She was far too good for this dump anyway.'

'Well, I don't want your opinion because I don't trust it,' said Alec furiously. 'And I don't trust you either,

Mr Kingsley. In fact, I'm not sure I believe a word you've said apart from the fact that you and Marie were having an affair. You see, she'd arranged to meet *me* the night she vanished, so how could she meet you as well?'

Mark Kingsley reached down to his left and pressed a buzzer. 'She was going to stand you up, Alec, like she usually did when I was free. I'd say you had more motive than me to want to get rid of her.'

Two large bouncers from the nightclub appeared in the doorway. 'Show this gentleman out, please,' said Kingsley calmly, all traces of rage now smoothed from his face, 'and memorize his face. He's no longer welcome here, and nor is the girl he's with.'

'Very good, Mr Kingsley,' replied the taller of the two and the next moment Alec was being hustled outside on to the High Street pavement where his arms were released and he found himself standing next to a nervous looking Tess.

'Are you all right?' she asked anxiously.

He rubbed his arms. The men had been strong and he could feel the impressions of their fingertips. 'I've been worse, but I've been better!' he admitted ruefully. 'At least I got him to admit it though. Patsy was right; Mark Kingsley *was* Marie's secret lover.'

'How did you get him to admit that?' asked Tess in astonishment.

Alec noticed that the two bouncers were still standing in the doorway watching them. Putting an arm round Tess he guided her away from the nightclub. 'We'd better not talk here; we've definitely outstayed our welcome.'

'But how did you make him confess?' persisted Tess, once they'd reached the end of the road.

'Simple. I relied on his greed and asked if he could sell me a watch for my girlfriend. A nonexistent, older woman with money,' he added with a laugh.

'And?'

'And then he produced a watch

exactly like the one you described your father finding in your room. The watch that we were almost certain her boyfriend had given her. Once I told him we'd seen Marie's watch he gave in without a struggle.'

'You're brilliant!' exclaimed Tess, and without thinking she flung her arms round Alec and kissed his cheek before quickly stepping back, pink in the face with embarrassment. 'Sorry!' she apologized quickly.

Alec grinned at her. 'No need to be; I enjoyed it, even if I didn't do very much to deserve it. The thing is, although I got him to admit it he made it pretty clear that if you or I tried to pass that information on to anyone else we'd regret it.'

'But that proves he's exactly the kind of man who could kill!' said Tess in horror.

'Possibly, although threatening people and killing them aren't the same thing by any means. Besides, we don't know that anyone's killed Marie. Like most other people, Mark Kingsley seems to believe she's run off to

London.'

'Why?' demanded Tess.

'He says she was too good for this dump. A bit rich, that, when you think that he's trying to make a lot of money out of the same "dump". It doesn't make much sense in another way either. Apparently Kingsley had originally intended to meet Marie that night when she finished work but at the last minute he couldn't. It doesn't seem likely to me that she'd have been planning to catch a late night train to London if she was expecting to meet with either her secret lover or, failing that, me.'

'I don't understand any of it,' complained Tess as they made their way through the small shopping precinct towards a coffee shop that stayed open until midnight. 'I mean, she'd rung me and was definitely going to stay up to give me this exciting news. She also said she was meeting Kingsley the next night, so he must have changed their plans before she rang. But she still had you waiting for her, so where did she go? Why didn't anyone see her from the moment she stepped out of the doors of the Skylark Motel?'

Once they were sitting drinking coffee they turned it all over in their minds again.

'It would make far more sense if she hadn't been seen leaving the motel,' said Alec thoughtfully. 'If she'd slipped out of the back entrance then she wouldn't have been seen if anything had happened to her. There's only a small lane from the canal up to the motel grounds and no lights at all at night out there. It's a short cut to where I was waiting, and it would have been easy for her to have vanished.'

'But she *was* seen,' Tess pointed out. 'It was a definite sighting and the receptionist knew the time as well. We've done all we can for now. It's really down to Ian to see what he can find out about the motel. After all, whatever it was she was so excited about must have been something she saw or heard there.'

'Maybe, but not necessarily something connected with her disappearance,' said Alec gently.

170

'We're finding out an awful lot about her, and not much of it's what we want to hear, but nothing explains why she hasn't turned up.'

Tess put down her cup and when she looked at Alec, her face was pale. 'I think she's dead,' she whispered. 'I've tried and tried to tell myself it isn't true, that she's just gone off like they say and that we'll hear from her out of the blue, but I know that isn't the way it is. I *feel* that she's dead. I can't explain it, but there's a space—a hole—where she used to be.'

'You're tired and low,' said Alec, catching hold of her hand on the table. 'You won't feel like this in the morning.'

Tess blinked hard. 'I will. If you want the truth, Alec, I felt it that first night, even before Dad rang the police. I kept denying it, to myself as well as everyone else, but it's how I felt.'

'That's awful,' said Alec, his dark eyes soft with sympathy, and they sat together for a long time without speaking a word, their hands clasped tightly together.

＊　　　＊　　　＊

While Alec and Tess were in the coffee shop, Ian was busy in the lounge of the Skylark Motel, where once again a party of Keith Palmer's friends were drinking prior to taking a meal in the small private function room. He'd looked for Karen earlier, but without success, and when the businessmen finally went off to eat he asked another waiter, John, if he knew where Karen was.

'Haven't you heard? She's left,' replied John.

'Left? But why? She told me she liked it here and needed the money.'

John lowered his voice. 'I think she was sacked. Apparently Mr Palmer heard her talking to another waitress about some phone call she'd heard that missing girl making the night she vanished. She knew as we all do that we're not meant to discuss Marie, and it seems Mr Palmer gave her her cards.'

'If she overheard something important she should have gone to the

172

police before this,' said Ian.

John pulled a face. 'I doubt if it was important. After all, you wouldn't make an important call from a phone in the hallway of a motel, would you? No, she was probably gossiping to a friend, but that didn't make Mr Palmer any happier.'

'What doesn't make Mr Palmer happy?' asked Keith Palmer, suddenly appearing behind the two lads.

'When we don't keep the ashtrays clean,' said John quickly. As he spoke he picked up a cloth and advanced towards the table where Keith's friends had been sitting.

'It certainly doesn't,' agreed Keith, but Ian thought he looked suspicious. However, after a moment he turned his attention to Ian. 'I wondered if you could help out on Saturday?' he asked. 'I know you're due to have the day off but one of our kitchen staff's got the summer flu and won't be in. You're a good worker and it would be extra money for this European trip you plan to make. What do you say?'

'Sounds great,' agreed Ian, hoping

173

that working in the kitchen might mean he got a chance to talk to some different people about Marie.

'Right, I'll put you down for it then. Get here at five-thirty. You'll be free to go about midnight, and I'll pay you a bit over the odds for helping us out in a crisis. Can't say fairer than that, can I?' He smiled at Ian and Ian smiled back but he found it hard. He kept remembering what Karen had told him about Marie and Keith. He only hoped that Karen was safe.

When he left that night the men were still shut away in their private room, and he couldn't help noticing that one of the cars in the crowded car park was badly damaged with its front wing buckled, the blue paint heavily scratched. Another one for Alec's garage! he thought to himself.

On a sudden impulse he walked over to the car and started to examine it more closely beneath the bright lights of the car park. It was only a year old but filthy dirty, and when he ran his hand over the driver's door that too was dented.

'What do you think you're doing?' asked a strange voice, and Ian jumped as a large hand gripped his shoulder.

Turning his head, Ian saw that it was one of Keith Palmer's friends who was gripping him. He was a tall man, well over six feet in height and built like a heavyweight boxer. His complexion was pale and his eyes dark and tired looking while his mouth was tight with anger.

'I just came over to see how badly the car was damaged,' explained Ian, trying to free himself from the man's grip.

'What's it to you?' snarled the man.

'My mate works at the local garage. I thought he might be able to do something with it if the owner was staying here for a night or two,' gabbled Ian.

The man looked hard at him for a few seconds and then released his grip. 'Very thoughtful of you. As a matter of fact it's my car, and Keith's getting it fixed while I'm here.'

'How did it happen?' asked Ian casually.

'Some fool drove straight out of a side road and hit me,' replied the man. 'He was drunk, of course.'

'At least you'll get it paid for by his insurers then,' said Ian with a smile.

'What?' For a moment the man looked puzzled, but then he grinned. 'Yeah, sure, that's right. Nothing like a bit of insurance when things go wrong, that's what I say. Have you got a home to go to, or are you planning on spending the night here?'

Ian backed away, feeling decidedly nervous. 'No, I'm off now. Goodnight.'

The man didn't reply, but he watched carefully until Ian was off the premises of the Skylark Motel.

*   *   *

As soon as Ian got in he phoned Tess and told her all that had happened at the motel. 'What do you think?' he asked eagerly.

'About Karen or the car?' asked Tess.

'The car, of course.'

'I don't see what the car's got to do

with Marie. I'm more interested in the fact that Karen's been fired. Where does she live? One of us ought to go and speak to her, find out exactly what reason Keith Palmer gave for getting rid of her.'

'I think the car's more important,' said Ian. 'You remember Alec said he was getting a lot of repair work but that none of it was done on insurance? Well, if this one goes to him and isn't done on insurance then the man was lying.'

'So what if he was?' asked Tess. 'He probably didn't think it was any of your business what happened to his car. Maybe he was the one who was drunk? If a car comes out of a side turning it usually hits the passenger side, otherwise it's got to cross over the road for some reason, missing all the traffic coming the other way as well. Pretty unlikely, I'd have thought.'

'I think these cars *are* important,' said Ian. 'You should see Keith Palmer's friends! They're a very unsavoury lot.'

'But they didn't know Marie,' Tess

pointed out. 'We don't even know if any of them were there on the night she vanished.'

'I can find out,' said Ian eagerly. 'I'll try and check it with the bookings clerk when I do this extra shift on Saturday. How did your day go?'

Tess related all that had happened at the Take Four nightclub and Ian whistled when he heard that Mark Kingsley had admitted to an affair with Marie. 'You did well!' he exclaimed.

'It was all Alec's doing,' said Tess, and Ian heard a note of pride in her voice. 'He was terrific. I was getting really wound up so he got me out of the room and then trapped Mark with the watch.'

'He's certainly impressed you,' commented Ian, feeling a twinge of jealousy.

Tess felt awkward. She never liked talking over the phone when you couldn't see people's faces, but she knew that Ian was right. Alec had impressed her in more ways than one.

'Do you suppose there's any connection between Mark Kingsley and Keith Palmer?' asked Tess. It was an idea that had been troubling her for a while now and she used it as a way of changing the subject.

'I've no idea,' confessed Ian. 'But if there is, it isn't something anyone seems to know about. Although I'm told Mark sometimes ate at the Skylark, no one's said he spent any time with Keith Palmer.'

'It would make it all tidier,' said Tess. 'At the moment nothing we're learning gets us anywhere. If anything, everything we discover complicates things more.'

'I know,' agreed Ian. 'Sometimes I wonder if we're ever going to get at the truth. It's really frustrating. Are we going out tomorrow?'

'I've used up my allowance,' confessed Tess. 'Getting in to Take Four this evening took the last of it.'

'You mean Alec didn't pay for you?' asked Ian in surprise.

'He offered, but I wanted to pay my own way. After all, I'm not his girlfriend.'

'No,' said Ian. 'You're mine, and

don't you forget it!' he added with a laugh.

'What shall we do then?' asked Tess.

'Come round to my place. The parents are going out to friends so we'll have the place to ourselves. We can hire a video if you like, or listen to some music.'

'A video and a pizza,' declared Tess. 'It's about time we did something on our own, something just for fun. All we've done recently is chase around finding out about Marie.'

'I agree,' said Ian. 'It's time we thought about ourselves for once.'

When Tess replaced the receiver she went thoughtfully upstairs to bed. Ian was right; they hadn't thought about themselves very much at all lately, but whereas a few weeks earlier she'd been worrying about what she'd do when he went away, she found now that the idea didn't upset her so much, and she knew that the reason for this was Alec.

CHAPTER TEN

At seven o'clock the next morning, Tess was woken by the sound of the telephone ringing. She leapt out of bed and followed her father down the stairs. He was only just awake himself, and pulling his dressing gown cord tightly round his waist as he went.

'Hello?' he said tensely, and Tess knew that like her he was desperately hoping that such an early call meant news about Marie. 'Yes, Sergeant,' he continued, and Tess's heart started to race. She moved quietly down to the bottom step and then sat with her arms round her knees watching her father's face closely. He was pale, and gripped the receiver tightly, but his words didn't tell her as much as she needed to know.

'I see,' he kept saying. 'Yes, quite. I understand.'

I don't! thought Tess to herself. *Hurry up and finish. I want to know what's happening.* At the top of the stairs her mother was waiting too, but she couldn't make herself come down. At last Tess's father thanked the police sergeant one final time and replaced the receiver.

'Well?' demanded Tess, getting to her feet. 'What did he have to say? Is there some news? Has someone seen Marie?'

He looked up the stairs to where his wife was waiting. 'No, I'm afraid no one's seen Marie. There's still no news about her at all.'

Tess heard her mother give a stifled cry and rush back into the bedroom. She stared at her father in astonishment. 'But if there's no news, why did they call you so early? Something must have happened.'

He nodded. 'Yes, something has. Kathy Robinson's been found.'

'Found? Is she all right? What happened to her? Does she know anything about Marie?' gabbled Tess.

Her father put an arm round her shoulders. 'Slow down, Tess. I told you, the police don't have any more information on Marie at all. They just wanted us to know that Kathy's been found safe and well in London before we heard the headlines on the radio. They think it will go something like "Missing girl found safe and well", and they didn't want us to hear that and get our hopes up, even for a few seconds. It was nice of them to ring,' he added.

'Nice?' demanded Tess angrily. 'How can you say that? They haven't been nice about Marie for a single moment. They haven't bothered to follow up any leads, apart from Alec not having an alibi. They're not interested in her married boyfriend, or her phone call from the motel. They just keep saying she's run off to London.'

'The trouble is,' said her father sadly, 'that it seems Kathy Robinson did exactly that. If someone hadn't recognized her from a picture in the local paper and told the police in London then she wouldn't have been found either. She wasn't intending to come home, Tess. The police probably feel more justified than ever in assuming Marie's done the same thing now that this has happened.'

'But I talked to Kathy about Marie,' persisted Tess. 'She seemed strange, really on edge. I'm sure she knows something about it all.'

Her father gave her a long, hard look. 'If that's the case then you'd better talk to the police about it. They've got Kathy at the station now. I'll call them and tell them what you've told me.'

He did, and as a result half an hour later Tess found herself facing a police inspector who was far less relaxed than the sergeant and WPC they usually saw. He too brought a policewoman with him, but she remained silent.

'Why did you go and talk to Kathy Robinson, Tess?' asked the Inspector after a few polite preliminaries.

'I've told you all this once before!' Tess protested.

'Yes, I know,' responded the Inspector. 'We just need to go over it one more time.'

'All right,' agreed Tess grudgingly. 'I went to see Kathy because she's a friend of Marie's and I thought she might know something.'

184

'You didn't think we might have talked to her?'

Tess pulled a face. 'How was I to know? You haven't seemed very anxious to talk to people. I mean, you didn't try and find out about her married boyfriend or anything, did you? Besides, even if you had talked to Kathy, there was a chance she'd say more to me than she would to you.'

'I'm sure there was. We've had great difficulty getting anyone to talk to us about your sister, Kathy, or the dead man in the fens. Stamfield people don't seem very anxious to help the police.'

'It's a small town,' explained Tess. 'Word gets around quickly here; no one wants to be thought of as the kind of person who tells tales.'

'Not even if someone's been murdered?'

Tess shook her head. 'He wasn't local, was he? No way are local people going to be interested in him. I thought they'd have talked about Marie and Kathy, but apparently I was wrong.'

He gave a half-smile. 'Not totally wrong. Contrary to what you seem to

185

think we have had a few leads to follow up regarding your sister's disappearance, but we'd have got on quicker with more public co-operation. Now, your father says you thought Kathy knew something about Marie's disappearance. Is that right?'

'Yes.'

'Why did you think that?'

'Because she wasn't friendly. She seemed nervy and on edge. We know each other very well. She and Marie were close. It didn't make sense to me, but the more I pushed her the more she shut me out.'

'She didn't say anything definite?' asked the Inspector. 'For example, she didn't say that she knew what had happened to Marie but couldn't tell you?'

'No! She kept saying she didn't know, but I was sure she was lying.'

'We've talked to her at some length since she got back early this morning,' said the Inspector. 'She still says she doesn't know anything about Marie, or where she might be now. However, the fact that Marie vanished did give her the idea of taking off herself. Kathy says that Marie was always complaining about being bored, and that they used to discuss how great it would be to live in a big city. When she heard that Marie had vanished she assumed she'd taken off out of boredom and decided that she'd do the same. She was annoyed that Marie hadn't confided in her.'

'But we don't know that Marie *did* take off,' protested Tess.

'I agree, we don't. What we do know now is that there's no link between your sister vanishing and Kathy Robinson disappearing, except for the fact that one incident triggered off the other. We can also safely assume that the reason Kathy was on edge when you spoke to her was because she was already planning her vanishing act and didn't want you to guess.'

Tess slumped back in her chair, disappointment all over her face. 'Do you really think that's what it was?' she asked.

The Inspector nodded. 'Yes, I'm afraid I do. Tess, we know how hard this is for you and your parents but we are working on it all the time. We're pretty sure she did the same as her friend Kathy, but not a hundred per cent certain, which means we *are* following other lines of enquiry. You've got to trust us. It's foolish to go blundering around trying to play detective yourself. Especially when one of your most helpful friends doesn't have an alibi for the night in question and is known to have dated Marie several times.'

'But Alec wouldn't hurt Marie!' protested Tess.

The Inspector rose to his feet. 'How can you be sure, Tess? Do you know something that we don't? Something that puts him in the clear?'

'No, of course I don't.'

'Then take my advice and be careful. Thanks for talking to us, and I'm only sorry we haven't got any news about Marie yet, but I'm sure we will have. Just give us time.'

Tess watched the police car drive away and knew that as soon as Kathy got home she had to go and see her. If she had seen Marie while she was in London she wouldn't have told the police but she would tell Tess, because she'd understand how much fear she'd caused her own family by disappearing into thin air.

*   *   *

Although Kathy's parents were trying to keep people away from her until some of the fuss had died down, after a talk with Tess's mother they agreed to let Tess see her that afternoon.

'She desperately needs to talk to someone about Marie,' her mother explained, 'and she's convinced that Kathy might know something.' Tess stood by the phone and wished that her mother would keep quiet about her feelings, but at least it got her what she wanted—a talk with Kathy.

There were a couple of photographers hanging around outside the Robinsons' house when she arrived, and Tess heard their cameras click as she walked up the front path. The door was opened just enough to

189

let her through without any of the Robinson family showing themselves.

'I wish those people would go away,' said Mrs Robinson, leading Tess through into the back room. 'What Kathy needs now is some normality. We don't want her getting lots of publicity over this. She ran away; that isn't clever or brave. She caused us a lot of worry and the police a lot of wasted time. She isn't a heroine.'

'I doubt if the police wasted much time,' said Tess shortly.

'They were very concerned,' said Mrs Robinson. 'I think that because she was the second girl to go missing they were forced to take it seriously.'

'Well, I wonder what they'll do about Marie now Kathy's back,' said Tess, walking into the small back room. Kathy looked up and attempted a smile, but her eyes were red-rimmed from crying. Mrs Robinson left the two girls alone together.

'You all right?' asked Tess, suddenly feeling awkward.

Kathy nodded. 'I feel a bit silly, to tell you the truth. It was horrible, Tess.

I hadn't thought it through at all. My money ran out after a day and a half and I had to spend one night sleeping out on a bench. It was awful. There were so many weird people wandering about. Then I got a job as a waitress at this really seedy café where they didn't ask any questions but they made you work awfully long hours and the money was pathetic. Trouble is, when you haven't got a penny you aren't in any position to make a fuss.'

'Why didn't you ring home?' asked Tess.

Kathy sighed. 'I felt so stupid. I'd run off without even leaving a note, thinking that I was going to have such a wonderful time, and then when I realized what it was really like I didn't want to let them know how stupid I'd been. I knew they'd go on and on about it for the next six months. Perhaps that's what's happened to Marie.'

Tess felt a twinge of sympathy for her, although she thought Kathy'd been pretty naïve to imagine she was going to walk into a good job without any references or qualifications.

'Were you planning to meet up with Marie?' she asked. 'Was that the idea? Had Marie told you she was going off to London and arranged for you to join her?'

Kathy shook her head. 'No, Marie never said anything to me about running away. She was always on about being bored and saying that she and I would fit in better in a big city, but she didn't once say she planned to go. Well, not until she'd finished her design course and could apply for a decent job.'

'So, why *did* you go?' asked Tess.

'Well, after Marie vanished I thought that she might have run off. I was annoyed that she hadn't told me—after all we were pretty close—and I thought that if I went off to London I might meet up with her and we could get a bedsit together or something.'

'Why London?'

'That's where Marie always wanted to work, so I assumed that would be where she'd gone, but I don't think that any more, Tess, not if I'm honest.'

Tess felt very angry. 'Why not? Just

192

because you didn't happen to see her while you were there? That's stupid. London isn't like Stamfield, as you must have noticed. You could both be there for months without bumping into each other.'

'I know that! No, the thing is, Marie wouldn't have done something so impulsive. She'd have thought it through and realized it couldn't have worked.'

'So, where do you think she is?' asked Tess.

'I've no idea,' admitted Kathy. 'The police interviewed me after she vanished, and then again last night, and they kept asking me the same thing, but I just don't know.'

'When I came to see you last time, you were very strange,' said Tess. 'I thought you were keeping something back. Surely you can be honest now?'

'The only thing I was keeping back was my plan to run off to London. I was afraid that if I said much I'd give it away. I was bursting to tell someone, and without Marie here you were a kind of substitute. I nearly did say once, which was why I got rid of you quickly.'

Tess felt utterly miserable. 'This means that we're no closer to finding out what happened to Marie, doesn't it?'

Kathy nodded. 'I'm sorry, Tess. I'd help if I could. Seeing how frantic my parents were while I was away, I'd love to help you and your family, but I can't. All I can tell you is what I told the police.'

'And what was that?' asked Tess.

'I said that Marie was very popular with the boys, and the men, come to that. She didn't have many close girlfriends, and quite a few of the other students at college were jealous of her, but none of them would have hurt her.'

'What about her married lover?' asked Tess, keeping her eyes on Kathy's face.

Kathy went red. 'The police asked about him, but I explained that although she talked about him she never gave me his name and I never saw them together. They probably don't believe me but it's the truth. You

194

know how close Marie could be. If she didn't tell you, why should she tell me?'

'Did the police seem to believe he existed?' asked Tess eagerly.

'Yes, they did. They also asked me if I could think of any local boy who might have had a grudge against her.'

'And I suppose you said Alec,' muttered Tess wearily.

Kathy's eyes opened wide. 'Alec? No, I didn't think of Alec. I know he and Marie went out together sometimes, but he isn't a possessive sort of person, is he?'

'So you couldn't think of anyone?'

Kathy looked down at the ground and fidgeted. 'Well, not really,' she mumbled.

'Come on,' said Tess. 'You've got to be honest with me. If you know something I don't, then tell me! It's my sister who's missing, remember?'

'Well, I said that Ian's never liked Marie much,' admitted Kathy, reluctantly.

'What?' Tess could hardly believe her ears.

'He never has liked her, Tess,' said

Kathy, raising her eyes to meet Tess's. 'Perhaps you haven't noticed but sometimes, when she's in one of her flirty, show-off moods and makes jokes at your expense, he gets very annoyed. He goes quiet and doesn't laugh like the rest of us do.'

'But that doesn't mean he'd hurt her!'

'I didn't say anything about him hurting her; I only told the police that he was the one boy I knew who wasn't bowled over by her. He hated the amount of influence she had over you, too.'

'How do you know that?' demanded Tess.

'I heard him telling Alec once that he couldn't understand why you didn't stand up to her more. Didn't he ever say anything like that to you?'

'Yes,' admitted Tess slowly. 'He has mentioned it now and again.'

'There you are then. I'm not making it up, and I'm not trying to cause trouble either, but it's the only thing I could think of that could possibly be of any help to them. I'm sure it doesn't mean anything, and they certainly didn't seem very impressed but at least I told them the truth for once.'

Tess stood up. Suddenly she wanted to get away.

'Right, well that's it, then. I'll be going now. Your mum didn't want me to stay too long. I'm glad you got back safely,' she added.

'So am I. I shall appreciate Stamfield more for a bit now!' Kathy watched Tess walk to the door.

'Tess!' she called.

'Yes?' queried Tess, turning her head.

'As a matter of interest, why didn't you stand up to Marie more?'

'I had my reasons,' said Tess, anxious to be gone.

'It was that Jean-Paul, wasn't it? You were afraid Marie would tell Ian about him.'

Tess stared at her in astonishment. 'How do you know that?'

'Because Marie told me, of course— about Jean-Paul, I mean. Not that she threatened to tell Ian about him—I worked that out for myself.'

'But she told me she'd never let anyone know!' exclaimed Tess.

'Yes, well, Marie wasn't the most reliable person in the world, was she? Don't worry, Tess—your secret's safe with me.'

As Tess hurried out of the house she found that she was furiously angry. 'How could you, Marie?' she muttered to herself as she walked towards her home. 'Couldn't you keep anything secret apart from your own affair?'

It seemed not, and now Tess wondered if this was why her sister had vanished—because she couldn't keep a secret. As for what Kathy had said about Ian, she pushed that firmly to the back of her mind. It was nonsense, and she wasn't going to consider it for a moment. The trouble was, that was easy to think, but not so easy to do.

CHAPTER ELEVEN

'Good pizza,' murmured Ian, snuggling up to Tess as they sat on the sofa in his front room. She nodded and wiped the last of the sticky mozzarella cheese off her fingers with a piece of kitchen paper. 'Good video, too. I think Sean Connery's gorgeous.'

'He's old!' laughed Ian. 'A pensioner! How can you fancy a pensioner?'

Tess laughed back. 'He's got more sex appeal now than you'll ever have, Ian Groves. Let's face it, you've either got it or you haven't and Sean Connery most definitely has.'

'How about Alec?' asked Ian, quietly.

Tess stopped laughing and stared at him in surprise. They'd been having such a good time. They'd managed not to mention Marie the entire evening and now he was spoiling things. 'What do you mean?' she asked.

'I wondered if you, like most of the girls round here, think Alec has sex appeal, that's all. It's not a difficult question to answer, is it?'

'No, it's easy. Of course he's got sex appeal, but so have you, really. I was only winding you up.'

'You like him a lot, Tess, don't you?' continued Ian, never taking his eyes off her.

Tess, who'd been sprawled across half the sofa, pulled herself into a sitting position. 'What is this? The Spanish Inquisition?'

'It's a question, that's all. You've spent a lot of time with him lately. Most girls think he's fantastic and I thought you might have fallen for his charm and good looks as well.'

'He isn't only good looking, he's a genuinely nice guy,' said Tess crossly. 'And it isn't his fault if loads of girls fancy him. Loads of blokes fancied Marie but I never blamed her for that.'

'Do you fancy him, Tess? That's what I need to know,' asked Ian.

'No, not in the way you mean. I like him, we get on well and he's been incredibly supportive over Marie but it's not, you know, *special*. It wouldn't be, would it? He's got loads of girlfriends. I don't think he thinks of me as anything more than a friend.'

Even as she spoke Tess knew that she wasn't being truthful. Alec's touch and the way he'd looked at her the previous night after they'd been thrown out of the nightclub had made it plain that she was far more than a friend to him now.

'I see,' said Ian slowly.

'Happy now?' asked Tess, moving closer to him. It wasn't as though she'd gone off Ian, she thought to herself, it was just that they hadn't seen enough of each other lately.

He sighed. 'I'm confused, Tess. This business of Marie is really getting to me. I dream about her, and it's all I seem to talk about when I'm awake.'

'Why does it upset you so much?' asked Tess slowly. 'After all, she's my sister, not yours. And you didn't even like her much, did you?'

Ian stared at her. 'What's that supposed to mean?'

'Well, you were always telling me I let her boss me about too much. And although you liked looking at her legs you didn't think she was as nice as most of the other guys did. She never made you laugh for a start.'

'That's because her jokes were often

201

jokes at other people's expense. I don't think that's very clever. Look, what is this? You sound as though I've done something wrong just because I say she's on my mind a lot. Don't you dream about her?'

'Yes, all the time; but like I said, she's my sister. I'm surprised you're so upset, that's all,' said Tess, realizing that she'd been affected by what Kathy had told her.

'I don't know why,' admitted Ian. 'I think it's tied up with waiting for my exam results and worrying about you and Alec getting into danger when I'm not there. Quite honestly, I've had enough of the whole thing: Marie's disappearance, the murdered man, the way the police won't tell us what they're doing. As soon as my results come through I'm leaving here. I'm not waiting until October, I'm going the first moment I can.'

Tess quickly moved away from him again until she was sitting at the far end of the sofa. 'You mean, Marie's not only vanished, she's also managed to split us up as well?' she demanded.

Ian shook his head. 'No, of course not. When I thought you fancied Alec I was sick with jealousy. I still care for you, Tess, but we're both young and I've got to get away from here. This place is driving me nuts.'

'What about me?' asked Tess. 'Where do I fit in? You don't want me fancying Alec but you don't want me to be with you either.'

'I do want you with me, but I suppose only until I leave,' admitted Ian.

Tess felt a lump in her throat and had difficulty in speaking. 'You mean, I'm a useful diversion until you can get away from Stamfield? Is that it?'

'Don't make me feel worse than I do already,' begged Ian. 'I know I'm being unreasonable, but at least I'm being honest with you. We both knew the score right from the start, didn't we?'

'Yes,' admitted Tess. 'It's so sad that things can't stay the same.'

'No, it isn't,' said Ian. 'It's good that they don't. Perhaps that's what Marie thought. Maybe everyone else is right and we're wrong. Maybe she did just pack up and go. Perhaps she couldn't face the goodbyes.'

'But she didn't pack up and go, she didn't pack a thing,' Tess reminded him. 'And anyway, I don't think you really believe that.'

Ian put his head in his hands. 'I don't know what I believe or think any more. I just wish Marie would waltz in your front door and say "Hi! I'm back. It was all a joke!" Then the rest of us could get on with our lives.'

'Sure, in a film that would probably happen,' said Tess, bitterly, 'but this isn't a film and I'd have thought that before you packed up and left us all behind, the least you could do was find that receptionist who saw Marie leave and try to have a few words with her. It isn't much to ask considering you're working at the very same motel she was.'

'But I can't find out the name of the receptionist that night. It isn't even in the book. I think it must have been a temp from an agency, or someone covering for a girl who was absent.'

'Well, find out,' said Tess sharply.

'There are two more weeks to go before the A-level results come through. It would be very nice if you could make some more progress before then, otherwise it will be up to Alec and me and we don't have access to inside information like you do.'

Ian reached out for one of Tess's hands. 'Tess, I'll do my best, I promise. And when I go I'll miss you horribly, but it's something I have to do. You can understand that, can't you?'

Tess gripped his hand and squeezed it gently. 'Yes,' she admitted finally. 'I can, but I'll miss you horribly too.'

'Look, the parents won't be back for ages yet. We can channel hop, see if there are any corny old films on TV or . . .'

'I'd like to go home now,' said Tess. 'It's been nice, but since we both know things are changing, there's not much point in me staying, is there?'

'I'd like you to,' said Ian.

Tess shook her head. 'Honestly, I'd rather go. What shifts are you doing this week?'

Ian checked his diary. 'I'm on

midday to four Monday and Tuesday, then I'm off Wednesday. Thursday and Friday I'm doing evenings and Saturday I'm helping out in the kitchen. That's probably the best chance I'll have of learning anything new about what happened to Marie.'

'It sounds as though you've got a pretty busy week,' said Tess as casually as she could manage. 'Why don't we wait, then meet up on Sunday and thrash things out? If by then you haven't got any further, and neither have Alec and I, you might be right and we're going to have to give up. Or at least you and Alec may have to give up. I shan't ever stop until we know what's happened to Marie.'

At the front door Ian put his arms round Tess and she relaxed against him, knowing that they were both aware their romance was nearing its end but helpless to change anything. 'Be careful where Mark Kingsley's concerned,' he cautioned her as they parted. 'Don't go near him on your own. He could be dangerous.'

'You be careful too,' said Tess. 'Just

make sure Keith Palmer doesn't find out you're asking questions or you'll end up like Karen—out of a job.'

*   *   *

The following afternoon Tess mooched down to the garage and found Alec hard at work in the repair shed. He had a car up on a ramp and she watched him for a few minutes before he became aware that she was there. His short-sleeved T-shirt and tight jeans emphasized his muscular build, and with his dark hair dishevelled and unruly he made her heart miss a beat with excitement. Surprised by her reaction she cleared her throat and he turned round.

'Tess! What are you doing here? I thought anything mechanical bored you!'

'Ian saw a car that had been pranged at the motel the other night. He wondered if it had been brought in here for repair.'

'What kind of car?' asked Alec.

'I think he said blue,' replied Tess

207

innocently.

Alec laughed. 'I meant make!'

She sighed. 'I don't know. A car's just a car to me. Ian might have mentioned it but it wouldn't have meant anything to me. I know he said the driver's side was badly damaged and a lot of paint had been scraped off.'

'I know the one,' said Alec, wiping his hands on a piece of rag and crossing the concrete floor towards her. 'It's over here. A man brought it in this morning. He wants it done by next Saturday morning. Cash on the nail, no insurance company involved, as usual.'

Tess frowned. 'That's odd. Ian spoke to the owner of the car and he claimed that he'd been hit by a drunken driver and said the repairs would be paid for by the other driver's insurance company.'

Alec went into the small office and checked through the entry book. 'No, it's quite definite here. He'll pay when he collects it. I took a quick look at the car and it's certainly had a hell of a knock. Did the owner say how it happened?'

'The second car came out of a side road without the driver looking,' replied Tess.

'And hit the driver's side? That's unusual.'

'Ian said that, too. But why would anyone lie about something like that?'

'More to the point, why pay for repairs if an insurance company can do it for you?' said Alec. 'It's going to cost a lot to get that thing roadworthy again. If someone else should be paying I can't believe the owner would want to pay cash himself. There's no sense in it.'

Tess followed Alec back to the repair shop and hesitated outside the entrance. 'What do you think it all means, Alec?'

'I haven't a clue but there's something odd going on. The question is, does it have anything to do with Marie's disappearance?'

'I don't really see how it can. Ian hopes to find out more on Saturday. He's working with different people on an extra shift and plans to ask some

209

questions then.'

'Saturday night?' asked Alec. Tess nodded. 'You'll be on your own again. Why don't we meet up when I finish work and go out somewhere? I finish about seven. If you can get yourself here by then I'll try and borrow a car off the boss and we can go for a spin. Or failing that,' he added with a grin, 'we could go on my motorbike.'

Tess shuddered. 'I'm never going on any motorbike. I loathe the things. They're noisy, uncomfortable and dangerous.'

Alec held up his hands in mock surrender. 'OK, a car it is! What are you doing this week? Seeing Ian much?'

Tess shook her head. 'No, he's working most of the time. I'm going to talk to more of Marie's friends, try and find out any extra details I can, and the rest of the time I'll probably catch up on seeing some of my own friends.'

'You and Ian ...' said Alec slowly. 'You haven't fallen out, have you?'

'He'll be off on his trip round Europe soon,' said Tess. 'I think in his mind he's already on his way, but we haven't quarrelled or anything. It's just the way things go.' She tried to be down-to-earth about it but her voice wobbled.

'Pity,' said Alec. 'You made a good couple.'

'People change,' said Tess sadly. 'We both knew this would happen, but for some reason Marie vanishing seems to have pushed us apart rather than brought us together.'

'Well, I'm not going anywhere,' retorted Alec. 'If you need to talk things over you know where I work and you know where I live.'

'Thanks,' said Tess, 'but if you don't hear from me in the week, I'll definitely take you up on the offer for Saturday.'

'Great. See you then,' said Alec, with a smile. He was still smiling when he started working again.

CHAPTER TWELVE

Working in the kitchen was far harder than Ian had expected. For a start it was hot, and everyone except him seemed to know exactly what they were doing. It didn't help that he had no idea of where anything was kept, or that no one made any allowance for this.

'Icing sugar shaker!' shouted a pastry chef at him. Ian hesitated, uncertain as to where to look. 'In the top cupboard, far left,' the chef called with a sigh. 'Honestly, we'd be better off without anyone if you can't do better than this.'

'I'm very sorry but no one's told me where anything is,' said Ian, feeling hot and sweaty.

'Trouble is, Mr Palmer's got a party of friends coming in later and we were already booked solid so I guess he thought we should be at full strength,' said the pastry chef, taking the shaker from Ian's hand.

'What's your name?' he asked, as he

got Ian to put large strawberries into dark chocolate cases.

'Ian Groves. I usually work as a waiter in the lounge bar.'

'You probably know my sister Karen, then. She used to work as a waitress here.'

'Yes, I know Karen,' said Ian eagerly. 'How is she?'

'Fine. She's working in a dress shop at the moment. She's happier there. I think she went off night work after those two girls vanished. Mind you, the one who worked here was a two-faced madam. Always flirting with the boss and telling tales on the other girls behind their backs. If anything has happened to her she probably asked for it.'

Ian felt himself growing red with fury but hoped the chef would put it down to the heat. 'You wouldn't think like that if it was Karen who'd vanished, would you?' he asked.

'Suppose not. Hadn't thought about it. I mean, it's not Karen, is it? Besides, Karen isn't the same sort of girl.'

There was no answer to such

indifference and Ian carried on working on the strawberry desserts.

'Petra didn't like her either,' said the chef, after a short pause.

'Petra?'

'Yeah, Mr Palmer's girlfriend. She could tell that Marie was keen on him. He even gave Marie a bottle of perfume once, that fancy stuff they go on about in books, what's it called?'

'Chanel No. 5?' asked Ian in amazement.

'That's right.'

'Keith Palmer gave that perfume to Marie?'

The chef narrowed his eyes. 'What do you mean? Did you know about it already? Are you here to work or to snoop?'

'I was just surprised,' said Ian quickly. 'My girlfriend wanted some of that stuff last Christmas but I couldn't afford it.'

The chef's face relaxed. 'No, but what's fifty quid to a guy like Keith Palmer? He's loaded, and so are those friends of his that come here. They leave huge tips, and sometimes they send money back to us in the kitchens as a thank you. Not many people think of doing that.'

'They sound a nice lot,' said Ian.

The chef laughed. 'I don't know about nice, but they're not short of a quid or two.'

A few minutes later Ian was moved and had to set to work peeling vegetables at one of the huge double sinks. After a time he was joined by a young, dark haired girl with a pale face and sullen air about her. Not much chance of a chat with her, he thought, but he was wrong.

'Were you a friend of Marie's?' she whispered suddenly, and Ian glanced nervously over his shoulder. 'It's all right, they're too busy to listen. Were you?'

'Yes,' he admitted.

'You see, there's something I know, something I've always felt I should have mentioned, but I really need this job and the money so when Mr Palmer said we weren't to talk, well, I didn't.'

'That's understandable,' Ian assured her.

'I saw Marie just before she made her phone call,' murmured the girl. 'She was standing in the passageway outside Mr Palmer's office and she looked as though she'd seen a ghost. Honestly, she was white as a sheet.'

'Christine!' shouted the head chef loudly. 'Stop chattering there and come and give me a hand straining this sauce.'

Ian continued peeling vegetables, but his hands were shaking as he thought about what this latest piece of information could mean. Marie must have seen or heard something that had scared her. It had scared her so much that she'd turned as white as a ghost and immediately called her sister. This had to be more than some small incident deliberately overdramatized by a teenage girl who wanted attention. It was something serious. But was it something so serious that Marie had had to vanish? he wondered.

'You, what's your name? The one peeling the potatoes,' shouted the chef.

'Ian,' he called back, his mind still on Marie.

'Right, Ian, get yourself out to the storeroom and fetch me two dozen frozen steaks.'

'Where's the storeroom?' asked Ian.

The chef sighed. 'I might as well do everything myself! Go out of the back entrance, turn left, and it's the second of the two doors on your right. Got that?'

'Out the back, turn left, then second on the right,' muttered Ian to himself as he dried his hands on a rather dirty towel. 'Won't be a moment.'

'Good. They'll want the steaks for dinner, not breakfast!'

Trying to ignore the laughter Ian hurried out of the kitchen and along the narrow corridor to the back entrance. He stepped outside and took a deep breath of the pleasant evening air. It was bliss after the stuffy kitchen. Then he turned left and in front of him saw two storerooms and to his right two large wooden doors which he assumed to be the entrances to the storerooms. To his surprise there was a notice on the second door that said 'Strictly Private', but although there was a heavy padlock threaded through the metal loop it was undone and after a moment's hesitation he removed it, placed it on the ground and walked inside.

The storeroom was very cold and there were two huge chest freezers set against the far wall. Neither of them was marked so he lifted the lid of the first and peered inside. At first he couldn't make out what he was looking at because it was covered in thick cellophane, but as his eyes adjusted to the gloom he realized that the whole chest was stacked full of wrapped bundles of banknotes. He had no idea exactly how much it was worth, but it had to be hundreds of thousands of pounds.

His heart began to race and his mouth felt dry. He knew now that he'd come into the wrong room. The chef had clearly given him the wrong instructions and he must get out of the place quickly, before anyone realized what he'd seen. Closing the lid of the freezer he began to walk towards the door, but then something made him stop, and as he turned and stared at the second freezer he felt the hairs on the back of his neck prickle and the coldness of the storeroom suddenly seemed to envelop his whole body.

Slowly, very slowly, he moved towards the second chest with his hand outstretched to open it. He didn't want to. He'd already seen more than enough to realize that there was something going on at the motel which the police should know about, but he couldn't stop himself. Despite his fear and the hammering of his heart in his chest he was driven on by a force greater than his own will. Finally his icy fingers closed around the handle of the lid of the second freezer and he forced himself to lift it and look inside.

Once again there was a lot of cellophane, but this time there were no banknotes inside. The cellophane was piled into an untidy shape, like a badly done up parcel, and in order to see what it concealed Ian had to lift the edges and try to peel it back. By now his hands were shaking so much that every movement was difficult and his legs were trembling as he listened out for the sound of anyone approaching the storeroom. The cellophane was thick and hard to handle but finally he loosened a piece and tugged hard on it. It was forced apart and the sudden movement dislodged the contents of the bundle. In a moment of heart-stopping terror that would stay with Ian for the rest of his life, a slim arm and hand shifted upwards and lay rigid on the edge of the freezer cabinet, fully exposed to his view. The hand was startlingly white, the nails perfectly shaped and painted a soft shade of pink, and on the smallest finger was a tiny gold snake ring with an imitation diamond for an eye. Ian recognized the ring only too well. Tess had bought it for Marie the previous Christmas, and Marie had liked it so much that she always wore it, no matter where she went.

Nausea rose in Ian's throat and for a dreadful moment he thought that he was going to be sick. He didn't dare stop and look at the body more closely because he knew that he had to get away. He had to run out of the storeroom, out of the grounds of the motel, and fetch the police immediately, before anyone realized what he'd discovered.

He could hear his own heavy breathing as he backed away from the terrible sight of Marie's body lying in the freezer and when he hit the door he turned and crashed through it, his legs hardly able to support him.

He wasn't looking where he was going, he was just running in a blind panic, racing for the path that led down to the canal and freedom. As a result he never saw the under-chef who'd been sent to find him until he cannoned into him. By now the full horror of what had happened had begun to dawn on him and he screamed aloud with shock at this unexpected encounter.

'What the . . . ? What's going on?' demanded the under-chef. 'Where are the steaks?'

'Get out of my way!' shouted Ian, twisting and turning as the other man caught hold of the cuff of his blazer.

'The steaks!' repeated the under-chef, who thought Ian must have gone mad.

'I didn't find ... It was the wrong storeroom ... Let me go!' yelled Ian, and at last he was free and fleeing for his life across the back courtyard towards the open fields.

Terror lent speed to his legs as adrenalin coursed through his veins, and although his lungs were labouring and every breath was agony as he drew nearer and nearer to the gates without hearing anyone behind him he was sure that he was going to make it. But then, at the last moment, as he raced through the back gates of the motel, Keith Palmer and three friends drove in through them.

Ian saw the car, swerved to avoid it and saw the faces staring out of the car windows at him. He knew how he must look, realized that the terror and shock must be clearly visible on his face, and tried to increase his speed. If the car turned and chased him he wouldn't have a chance, and he knew now that these men had already killed once.

There was no reason why they wouldn't kill again.

His legs were tiring and he was moving more slowly, so when he heard the scream of car brakes and the shouting of the men behind and realized that they were indeed going to come after him, he groaned in despair. If only he hadn't tried to do so much on his own! he thought miserably. He was quite alone, being pursued by a gang of ruthless killers, and there was no cover where he could hide. All he could do was keep running in a zigzag line, and that's what he did, even when he heard the first shot fly by his head.

CHAPTER THIRTEEN

At seven that evening, Tess had made her way to the garage to meet Alec, as arranged. She wasn't in the least surprised to find him still working, and for the first time allowed herself to admit that even if the mechanical workings of cars and motorbikes bored her there was no denying Alec's skill and dedication to his work.

He grinned at her. 'Won't be more than ten minutes, I promise. I got held up getting that car ready—the one Ian saw in the Skylark car park. By the time he'd collected it and we'd sorted out the bill I was behind on this one.'

'That's all right,' Tess assured him. 'I'm getting used to seeing you at work. I take it the man did pay cash?'

'He certainly did, and gave me a very generous bonus for getting the car repaired on time. Odd, isn't it?'

'Must be some kind of tax fiddle,' said Tess, confidently. 'Businessmen are always doing things like that, or so my dad says. Mind you, being a civil servant, he's biased!'

'There, that's done,' said Alec with satisfaction a little later. He slid out from beneath the car, wiped his hands on a towel and looked ruefully at his oil-covered overalls. 'I'll have to get these off and freshen up before we go. Do you mind waiting in the office? The boss said I could use his room to change.'

'No problem,' Tess assured him. 'Where are we going?'

'Fancy a trip to Nottingham? We could visit one of their nightclubs as we're banned from Take Four.'

Tess felt a flutter of excitement at the prospect of being seen out and about in Nottingham with Alec. 'Sounds great,' she said, in what she hoped was a suitably casual voice. 'I'll have to be back by midnight, though. Since Marie vanished, Mum and Dad have worried more.'

'I'm not surprised,' said Alec. 'Don't worry, I'll take good care of you and have you back promptly. Ian won't mind, will he?'

'Why should he?' asked Tess, picking up some keys from the desk and fiddling with them. 'He's made it clear that we're not an item any more and anyway he's working tonight.'

'Great. Be with you in a few minutes.'

While Alec was gone, Tess looked around at the usual calendars, posters and adverts that adorned most garage offices, and all the time she was

225

looking she continued to play with the bunch of keys that she'd found on the desk.

'Where did you get those?' asked Alec when he came back in.

Tess, who thought he looked great in a grey and white short-sleeved top and black trousers, frowned. 'Get what?'

'Those keys?'

'They were lying on the desk. Shouldn't I have touched them? Sorry, but I always fiddle with things. I chew the ends of my pencils too. Marie says it's a disgusting habit.' Her voice tailed off at the memory.

'You can do what you like with them,' Alec assured her, 'but I don't know where they come from. Keys are locked away when the garage is closed, and in any case I don't recognize those. Let me have a closer look.'

Tess held them out to him and their hands brushed lightly as he took them from her. She felt a spark of excitement run through her, but Alec was frowning, too busy examining the keys to notice her brightened eyes.

'Hey! These are a spare set of keys

for the car that's just been picked up. The guy must have forgotten them and he's leaving tonight—that's why I had to get the job done.'

'He'll have to come back for them then,' said Tess.

'He can't,' replied Alec. 'We'll be closed. I think we'd better take them up to the motel before we go out. We might even have a chance of a word with Ian before we leave.'

'OK,' agreed Tess, who quite liked the idea of Ian seeing that she wasn't moping round alone on a Saturday evening just because he was working. 'Which car are we using?' she added.

Alec pulled a wry face. 'Well, that's the bad news. I couldn't get a car; it's a motorbike or nothing, I'm afraid.'

Tess stared at him. 'We're going to Nottingham on a *motorbike*?'

Alec laughed. 'You sound as though I've suggested going on the back of a camel! Motorbikes are great. You get the most incredible buzz out of the feeling of the wind in your face, and the sense of speed's out of this world. I've got you a helmet, you'll be perfectly safe. Come on, Tess. Don't tell me you're chicken!'

'I just don't like them,' said Tess stubbornly.

Alec sighed. 'Then I guess we'll have to stay here and try to find something to do. Any suggestions?'

Tess racked her brains but they both knew perfectly well that there wasn't anything. There was a Disney film on at the cinema, all the pubs would be packed out, and most of their friends would be at the nightclub run by Mark Kingsley, which was out of bounds to them.

'You can wait here for me while I run the keys back,' said Alec. 'You'll be all right in the office, and then we can go to the bowling alley and have a Coke while we watch some of the league teams play if you want.'

Tess gave herself a mental shake. She wanted to go to Nottingham with Alec, and she knew that he was a careful driver. For once she would have to be more like Marie had been and show more spirit of adventure. 'No, I'll come too,' she said quickly. 'The only time I went on a motorbike was when I was going out with Frank Letts, and he scared me to death the way he drove it.'

'Frank's a total idiot,' said Alec dismissively. 'You'll enjoy riding pillion with me. Come on, give me the keys, then I'll lock up here and we'll drop in at the Skylark then whizz over to Nottingham. Should be a cool night out.'

At first Tess was nervous, but within a few minutes she found that she was enjoying herself. She had her arms clutched tightly round Alec's waist and once she'd got used to the sensation she realized that Alec was right—it did feel good. They drove along the road by the canal and then turned off on to the rough pathway that ran through the fields to the back entrance of the motel.

Tess's head was buried against Alec's back, so that when he suddenly jammed on the brakes and the bike skidded to a halt she was so taken by surprise she nearly fell off and lifted her head to see what was happening.

'Look!' shouted Alec, pointing ahead of them.

Tess stared in the direction of his hand and saw a figure in the distance running in a crazy jagged line through the fields, dodging first to the right and then to the left. She wondered if the person was being attacked by a swarm of bees.

'What's happening?' she asked Alec.

'I don't know, but that's the way Ian runs, and the guy's wearing white overalls or something. Wasn't Ian working in the kitchen tonight? They wear white there. You don't think it is him, do you?'

Tess narrowed her eyes, trying to make out the features of the running figure. It was drawing slowly nearer to them, and suddenly she was able to make out the face and knew that Alec's guess was right. It was Ian, but a very frightened Ian, whose face was twisted in what looked to be an expression of terror.

Even as they watched, a dark car raced out through the motel gates and started along the lane, driving parallel to Ian, and it was then that both Alec and Tess heard a sharp cracking sound rend the air.

'What on earth was that?' asked Tess.

'They're firing at him!' shouted Alec. 'Quick! We've got to get out of here and go for help before they see us.'

But Alec was too late. The occupants of the car had already seen them, and now the car accelerated towards them and there was another cracking noise as a gun was fired at them too.

'Hang on tight!' yelled Alec, revving up the bike. Tess, her eyes on the stumbling petrified figure of Ian, was a fraction too slow in responding to his order. As he spun the bike round ready to race back to town she grabbed for his waist, missed, and when he sped off down the dusty track Tess was thrown off the bike and lay wheezing and gasping on the edge of the field with all the breath knocked out of her.

Ian had seen the motorbike in the distance, and had even waved frantically at it to try and attract attention, but he didn't realize who the riders were, and when the car that had been chasing him accelerated and then stopped suddenly he was simply grateful for the distraction.

What he didn't realize was that one of the men had left the car and was now pursuing him on foot. The first Ian knew of this was when he heard pounding footsteps behind him, and then there was the sound of gunfire and a metre or so to his left a bullet hit the ground, throwing up a shower of dusty earth.

Ian stumbled in panic, and as he stumbled his foot got caught in a shallow dip in the ground so that his ankle turned and a sickening burst of pain flooded his foot, ankle and lower calf. He wrenched frantically at the trapped foot with his hands, but even when he got it free and tried to run again he found that it wouldn't take any weight and suddenly he was falling sideways until he, like Tess, hit the earth with a dull thud.

His pursuer's footsteps slowed as the man realized that there was now no need for haste. Ian was utterly helpless.

There was no longer any chance of him escaping. When the man drew level with Ian he grabbed hold of his shoulder and pulled him roughly upright, ignoring Ian's involuntary cry of pain as his twisted ankle was forced to take some weight.

'Shut up!' growled the man. 'You'll have more than this to shout about before Mr Palmer's through with you.'

'What have I done?' gasped Ian, his mind whirling as he tried to think if he could talk his way out of the situation. 'I was going home, that's all. It isn't a crime, is it? OK, so I was meant to work until midnight, but I'd had a row with my girlfriend and I wanted to—'

'I said, shut up!' said the man again, and he shook Ian so roughly that the pain in his ankle was almost unbearable. This time Ian took the man's advice and decided to save his defence for the moment when he and Keith Palmer came face to face.

In the meantime, Tess was being bundled into the back of the car by Keith and one of his accomplices. She was still finding it difficult to get her

233

breath and her ribs were aching where she'd hit the ground.

'Who are you? And who was your friend?' demanded Keith Palmer. 'And what were you doing here?'

'We were . . . It was just . . . He had some keys for you,' gasped Tess.

Keith Palmer's eye were hostile. 'Keys?'

She nodded. 'He works at Kays garage. One of your guests left a spare set of keys there this evening. We were bringing them back, that's all.'

'What a very civilized thing to do,' drawled Keith. 'The trouble is, your timing was off. You've seen too much for my liking. Unfortunate, but these things happen. Jim, has anyone gone after the lad from the garage?'

'Mick's going to try to cut him off at the far end of the lane,' replied the driver of the car, and Keith Palmer nodded in satisfaction. He glanced briefly at Tess again and then peered out of the window. 'Looks as though we've caught our absconding waiter. Better drive over and pick him up too, then we'll have to decide what we're going to do.'

'We'll have to get away,' said the driver, his voice tinged with desperation. 'We can't hang around here. Not if that lad's found you know what.'

'Yeah, well, let's not jump to hasty conclusions,' said Keith. 'We'll have a good chat to him when we get him back inside.'

Despite being dazed by her fall, Tess realized that the best thing she and Ian could do was pretend they didn't know each other. If Keith Palmer and his men didn't make any connection between them then it was just possible that they'd settle for tying them up while they made their getaway. Although exactly what Ian had learned that had made that necessary she couldn't think.

Unfortunately Ian, in shock after discovering Marie's body in the freezer combined with the burning pain in his ankle, didn't see the warning in Tess's eyes as he was thrown roughly into the back of the car with her and Keith Palmer, and he stared at her in wide-eyed astonishment. 'Tess! What are you doing here?'

'You mean you know each other?' asked Keith, his voice low and dangerous. 'That's very interesting. I thought you were a friend of the guy from the garage, young lady. How come you know this waiter of mine too?'

'Stamfield's a small town,' said Tess, in a bored tone. 'Everyone knows everyone else. We were at the same school.'

'What an interesting coincidence,' said Keith with a smile that didn't reach his eyes. 'The only problem is, I don't think I believe you.'

'Check the school roll then,' said Tess pertly.

'Oh, I believe you were at the same school, but for some reason I don't think it was a coincidence you were both here tonight.'

In an attempt to distract Keith, Ian gave a groan of pain. 'I think I've broken my ankle,' he moaned.

'Shame,' said Keith, unsympathetically. He turned back to

Tess. 'What's your name?'

'Tess.'

'Tess who?'

'Phillips,' she said automatically, and the moment the words were out of her mouth she knew that she'd made a terrible mistake. All the colour drained from Keith Palmer's face while Ian gave a muffled gasp of horror. 'What's wrong with that?' she asked defiantly.

'There's nothing wrong with it,' replied Keith. 'It's a very nice name, and a very familiar one. I've got a feeling I knew your sister, and she was a nosey-parker, too.'

CHAPTER FOURTEEN

The car drew up in a large wooden garage at the rear of the motel. Tess was grabbed by one of the men and Ian by another, then they were both dragged out and roughly manhandled into a cold, sparsely furnished room which had once been used as an outhouse. Tess shivered, partly from fear and partly from the drop in temperature.

To her terror, Keith Palmer walked over to where she was being held, her arms pinned to her sides, and, putting a hand beneath her chin, he tipped her face up so that she was forced to look him in the eye.

'You *are* Marie's sister, aren't you?' he asked her softly.

For a moment she considered lying to him, denying any knowledge of her missing sister, but something about the blank coldness of his eyes made her change her mind. She knew instinctively that it would make life easier for her if she told the truth. 'Yes,' she whispered.

'And this young man here, what's he to you?'

Tess hesitated, aware that only a couple of weeks earlier she would have automatically said boyfriend, but now, without her knowing it had happened, things were different. 'He's a friend,' she murmured.

'Do you mean a friendly spy?' demanded Keith, his fingers pinching

238

her skin hard so that she had a job not to cry out.

Tess tried to twist her head away. 'I don't know what you mean,' she stammered.

With an unpleasant laugh he released her. 'I think you do. I think the pair of you have been playing a clever game with me. Well, you made a bad mistake, as you'll find out very soon. Tie their hands and feet, then gag them both,' he told another of the men. 'Put them in the far corner while we work out what to do. We've got to act quickly. Whoever was driving that motorbike has probably gone for help. Luckily, knowing the local police, it will take him an age to persuade them there's anything out here they need to look at!'

Tess felt large rough hands tying cord around her wrists and ankles, and when she gave an involuntary cry of protest the cord was drawn even tighter and the man gave her a push that sent her stumbling awkwardly against the wall. She saw a man tying Ian up in the same way and then he too was thrown across the room and as he fell he hit Tess on the shoulder. 'Sorry,' he muttered.

'Don't worry,' whispered Tess.

Keith Palmer's head turned swiftly towards them. 'I said gag the pair of them!' he shouted angrily. 'Can't you lot do anything right?'

As a thick piece of linen was pushed into her mouth Tess felt her stomach heave and for a dreadful moment she thought that she was going to be sick, but she inhaled slowly and deeply through her nose to try and calm herself and at last the feeling passed.

'If they stay they'll hear what we say,' pointed out the man who'd tied Tess up, jerking a thumb in the direction of the two trussed teenagers.

'So what?' demanded Keith. 'They won't live long enough to talk. Get on with it.'

Tess heard the words and her stomach lurched. She felt her heart beating hard against her ribs while a tightness constricted her throat.

She turned her head to look at Ian and was startled to see an expression of resignation on his face, almost as though he'd already suspected they'd be killed. Then she remembered that the gang had already been trying to kill him when they fired at him as he ran from the motel. She wondered what on earth he could have discovered that had made his death necessary.

She didn't have to wait long to find out.

'Right,' continued Keith. 'First of all, we've got to get the money and the body away. Without that the police won't have a thing to go on.'

Tess knew then. At the mention of the word 'body' she guessed straight away that they were talking about Marie, but although she guessed it she didn't want to believe that she was right, and once again she looked to Ian for reassurance.

Ian wasn't able to give her any. As soon as Keith spoke, Ian remembered the dreadful sight of Marie's frozen blue-white corpse in the freezer, and the carefully manicured hand hanging over the side. When he felt Tess's gaze on him he hung his head and stared down at the stone floor. He couldn't comfort himself, let alone Tess, and he was ashamed of his own weakness.

'Where's the body now?' demanded a fair-haired member of the gang.

'In the freezer next to the one where the money's stashed,' replied Keith. 'Nothing's gone right from the moment that girl died. She should have been dumped miles away from here. If that car hadn't broken down she'd never have been kept in Stamfield. I knew it was risky shoving her in the freezer, even though the police had done their search.'

Tess curled herself up into a small ball, trying to protect herself from the terrible things that she was hearing. She concentrated hard on Alec, picturing him driving back into Stamfield and going directly to the police station. Surely they'd come out quickly? she thought to herself. Even if they weren't certain he was telling the truth they'd have to check out his story. 'Hurry, Alec! Hurry!' she muttered to herself behind her gag.

Keith Palmer walked over to one of

his men. 'Get the blue car loaded. Put the body in the concealed hollow in the boot and cover it with boxes of provisions from the motel's storecupboard. The money had better be hidden in green garden rubbish bags and put in the large van along with some bags that *do* contain rubbish. If we get some luck for once we just might get away with it still.'

'You were lucky it was Petra on duty at the desk the night you had to kill Marie,' commented a tall man who seemed to be second in command.

At this open confirmation of her worst nightmare Tess gave a muffled wail of despair and horror and for a brief moment all the men in the room turned to look at her. Then they quickly looked away again, and in their faces she read the bitter truth. They knew that very soon she too would be dead.

'I wouldn't call it lucky,' snapped Keith, his nerves plainly on edge. 'If Marie hadn't been standing outside my office door when Greg shot Luke for grassing on the rest of the London

243

gang then she'd never have had to die and none of this mess would have happened. The last thing we needed was another death.'

'It's your fault,' said the dark-haired man in an angry voice.

My fault? How do you work that out?' asked Keith softly. Tess felt herself begin to tremble again at the menace in his tone.

'You encouraged the girl in the first place. You were flattered by the fact that she thought you were some kind of macho hero, and you fancied her rotten yourself. That's why Petra was willing to say she'd seen her leave the motel. She was glad to see the back of the opposition.'

'She offered herself to me on a plate,' protested Keith, glancing across at Tess as he spoke.

Tess wished that her hands were free so that she could put them over her ears and blot out all the horrible words she was hearing. She could hardly believe that it was her sister Keith was talking about—that not only had Marie been going out with a married man, she had carried on with a second man at the same time. She realized that she'd never really known her sister at all, and that hurt. The greater hurt, the knowledge that she'd never see Marie again, she pushed to the back of her mind because right at this moment she simply couldn't deal with it.

'Nearly finished,' announced the man who'd gone out to load the car. 'It's a pity we've got to move on. This place was the perfect cover. No one thinks of London gangs laundering their money in the wilds of the Lincolnshire fens. Or of dumping the bodies of their grasses there either, come to that. The garage was useful too. All our cars were repaired and on their way back to London as good as new almost before their description was out on the police radios. A nice new set of licence plates and no more trouble. That boy was good. Now we've got to find somewhere else.'

Tess's heart sank as she heard the man praise Alec. She'd been pinning all her hopes on him getting to the police station quickly, but suddenly she understood that Alec himself could be involved with Keith Palmer.

After all, it was their cars that had been going to the garage, their cars that Alec had given up his free time to repair. And then, Alec had been free on the night Marie vanished. They only had his word that he'd been waiting for Marie. He could have been here, in this very motel, and known all along what had happened to her. His apparent helpfulness might really have been just a clever diversion, leading Marie and Ian away from the truth. If that was true, if he was involved and had been well paid for his part in their activities, then he certainly wouldn't go to the police. Should she and Ian die, no one would know that Alec had seen anything today. He could say that he'd been working at the garage, and although there'd be no witnesses there'd be nothing to link him with the motel either. It all made dreadful sense, and Tess desperately wanted to cry.

'Well, don't blame me,' said Keith aggressively, breaking into her thoughts. 'How was I to know I'd got a spy in my motel? Take the gag off him a minute. Before he dies, I want to know what put him on to us.'

Ian was pulled to his feet, the gag snatched from his mouth, and all he could think of as he faced Keith Palmer was that he must play for time. The longer he could keep the man talking the more chance Alec had of getting help to them, but with the combination of shock and pain he had trouble concentrating. Unlike Tess, he still had faith in Alec.

'Well?' demanded Keith. 'Why were you suspicious of the motel?'

'I wasn't,' said Ian quickly. 'The only reason I wanted to work here was to try and find out more about Marie. This was the last place she was seen alive so it seemed the best place to start looking for information.'

'And who on the staff was the most helpful?' enquired Keith with interest.

'No one. I'm sure some of them could have helped a bit but they wouldn't. They said they weren't allowed to talk about Marie.'

'Quite right,' approved Keith. 'I got my message across!'

'I think he's lying,' said a man behind Ian. 'He came here looking for something definite. Let's face it, Marie was a busy girl. He could have started his enquiries at lots of other places, among her friends or at the nightclub owned by her boyfriend. Why come here first?'

'It was because of the telephone call,' admitted Ian, knowing that Tess could hardly be in more trouble than she was already. Also, by telling the men this he could keep the conversation going.

'What phone call?' demanded the man. Keith looked uncomfortable so Ian rushed on with his story, hoping he might get the two men to quarrel and waste even more time.

'Marie rang Tess,' he explained. 'On the day she vanished she called her and said she had something incredible to tell her that night. She even offered to wait up until Tess got in late, which wasn't like Marie. Marie expected other people to wait up for her.'

248

'Something incredible? Is this true, Keith? Did that girl actually make a telephone call *after* she'd accidentally seen Luke killed?'

'I didn't know she'd seen him killed at first,' said Keith hastily. 'It was only when I heard a noise outside, went into the corridor and saw her hurrying away that I guessed she must have done. She went straight to the phone before I could speak to her. Luckily, when she realized other people were around she ended the call quickly. After that it only took me a minute or so to persuade her she was wrong and get her back into my office.'

'But she could have been calling the police!' shouted the man. 'Did you think of that?'

'Of course I did! I got Greg to get Luke's body away in his truck and dump it in the fens straight away, and then I kept Marie alive for an hour until I was sure the police weren't going to come calling. I chatted her up, pretended that what she thought she'd seen and heard was only an argument, but once I was certain the law weren't coming out here I stopped trying to kid her. There wasn't any point. I knew she didn't believe me, but why she called her sister instead of the law I'll never know.'

'Shock probably, and damned lucky for us!' snapped the man.

'Yeah, well, it wasn't easy killing her,' said Keith.

'What about this boy? Who's he been talking to during his unofficial enquiries?'

Ian had been listening to the men through a haze of pain and terror, grateful for the fact that with every passing moment his and Tess's chances of being saved were increasing. Now, when the voices stopped, he realized that he was expected to say something, but he'd lost the sense of the conversation and stared blankly at Keith.

Keith Palmer's eyes were quite indifferent as he drew back an arm and slapped Ian hard round the face. At the sound of the palm of his hand against Ian's flesh, Tess cringed and tried to make herself even smaller.

Ian's face burnt at first, and then began to throb, but he kept silent.

'Come on, Ian. Tell us who you talked to. I can make you talk quiet easily, but I'd rather not have to hurt you, not in front of your friend.'

'Only Tess,' said Ian, his cheek scarlet with the imprint of Keith's hand. 'We're . . . well, we used to go out together. That's how I got involved. I wanted to help her because she didn't think the police were doing enough. I'd have liked to talk to other people, but no one in this town seems interested in Marie any more. They all think she's run away to London.'

'I'm not sure that's true,' interrupted the dark-haired man. 'They must know something about Luke by now and could make a connection. Let's get the hell out of here while we can. I'll deal with the boy, you kill the girl. You've had the practice,' he added maliciously.

Tess began to shake uncontrollably. She felt a terrible coldness seep into her bones as though she were already dead. Keith Palmer stared at her indifferently. 'Sure, no problem,' he

251

agreed and Tess felt her eyes prickling with tears.

She didn't want to die! She was too young, and had her whole life ahead of her. She wished that she'd never begun all this, never insisted on finding out for herself what had become of Marie. The police had been right to try and warn her off. Worst of all, she'd never know the truth about Alec.

'You won't get away with it!' shouted Ian frantically. 'No one will believe that Tess and I have run off to London. You can't hope to dupe the police the same way a second time.'

'We don't intend to try,' snarled Keith. 'We'll hide your bodies in the freezer for them to find, but by the time they do we'll be gone. We've got a plane laid on and false passports ready. By the time your wonderful local force have got on our trail we'll be long gone and there's no way they'll ever find us.'

Ian knew then that there was no hope. These men were totally ruthless, and with their escape carefully planned they had no need to keep him and Tess alive a moment longer.

Keith Palmer drew a gun from beneath his jacket and turned Tess away from him. That meant she was facing the door and when he shot her he wouldn't be looking into her eyes.

'I'm sorry, Tess,' said Ian. 'I never meant you to get involved here.'

She wanted to tell him that it didn't matter, that she was sorry too and it wasn't his fault, but she still couldn't speak and she stood waiting, listening for the sound of the trigger being pulled back.

'OK,' said Keith. 'This is it!' and she heard the faint click that she'd been waiting for.

'Please, don't kill her!' cried Ian, but Tess knew the words were useless and at the last moment she stopped trembling and managed to straighten herself up. A strange sense of calm spread through her as she prepared to die.

CHAPTER FIFTEEN

The earsplitting crash of the door being kicked in astonished everyone in the room. Tess heard a man's voice shout 'Get down!' and she obeyed instantly, throwing herself on to the hard floor and trying to roll at the same time because her tied hands stopped her from breaking her fall. Quick as she was, she wasn't quite quick enough and a bullet from Keith Palmer's gun hit her in the right shoulder, but at the time she didn't realize as all the breath had been knocked out of her and she struggled to take in air, making hideous wheezing noises.

All she was aware of was the sound of shouting—men's voices yelling as those inside the room tried to escape, either through the windows or by shooting at the policemen, while outside in the motel courtyard two of the gang tried desperately to start up the blue car and the Transit van.

As bullets flew, and cries of pain

254

started to mingle with shouts of rage, Tess remained face down on the floor, waiting for someone to help her up once it was all over. But when hands eventually reached down to her they weren't gentle, reassuring ones, but rough and aggressive.

'I've got the girl!' shouted Keith Palmer, above the general chaos. The two police gunmen froze in their tracks as he hauled Tess to her feet. Then, keeping her in front of him as a human shield, he edged from the room and out into the courtyard.

Now the pain of the bullet wound really began to make itself felt and Tess had to bite her lip as she was hustled towards a locked garage where Keith kept his silver Jaguar.

She could see everything so clearly, it was almost like watching a film. Policemen were everywhere, all now standing helpless as the scene unfolded in front of them. In the kitchen doorway two members of the motel staff were standing staring, their mouths open with shock, but what Tess saw most clearly of all was Alec.

He was standing by one of the parked police cars and he was watching her intently, his tall muscular frame taut with tension as Keith took care to keep her between him and the policemen every step of the way.

As relief rushed through Tess, everything was blotted out except for Alec. She kept her eyes glued to him, and although she was too far away to make out his features she found that she could picture them very clearly: his black hair, falling in a stray lock over his right eye, and the eyes themselves, a dark, compelling blue.

At that moment, as she realized that he wasn't involved and she'd been right to trust him, Tess knew that she loved him. That during the past few weeks, as they'd worked together and tried to solve the mystery of Marie's disappearance, she'd slowly come to appreciate all his good qualities: his honesty, his bravery and above all his understanding of how she felt and why she was so driven to learn the truth.

Well, she thought to herself, now she knew it and the chances were she was going to die for her pains but at least the gang weren't going to get away with it. Neither she nor Marie would have died in vain. It was scant comfort, but better than nothing.

'Come on!' said Keith urgently, his left hand tight round her waist. 'Keep still, will you? I've got to unlock the garage door.'

Suddenly hope surfaced in Tess. She might be in pain, but unless Keith killed her, in which case he wouldn't have a hostage, he couldn't do anything much to make her keep still.

The moment she realized this she started to kick. She kicked backwards, and felt the heel of her shoe connect with his shinbone. When he gave a sharp cry of pain she wriggled and twisted in his grasp and then kicked again.

For a brief second Keith relaxed his grip and immediately Tess dropped to the ground like a stone and as she fell she heard a shot from a police marksman. With a scream Keith Palmer spun round, scrabbled at the thick wooden garage doors for a few seconds and then slid down to the ground next to her.

Tess didn't wait to see how badly he was hurt or if he was capable of using his own gun again. She simply got to her feet and ran as fast as she'd ever run in her life towards the waiting Alec.

Around her the scene slowly came to life again. With Keith Palmer down the other men seemed to lose heart, with the exception of one who was still fighting and cursing with two policemen. At last the entire gang were led into the waiting police van, while Keith Palmer was placed in the back of an ambulance, his face pale above the red blanket.

Tess wasn't aware of any of that. All she was aware of was the warmth of Alec's embrace, the strength of his arms around her and the wonderful words he was whispering in her ear before a policewoman came and led her gently away towards another ambulance waiting to take her and Ian to hospital for treatment for shock and injuries.

'I'll see you soon,' promised Alec as the ambulance doors closed behind her. Tess nodded, too full of emotion to speak, but she was able to use her eyes to show exactly how she felt.

A Detective Inspector came over to where Alec was standing. 'Sorry we doubted you for a moment,' he said briefly. 'I'm afraid Mr Palmer had us all fooled. He was the one who told us Marie was always talking about going off to London. With the rest of you saying how bored she was in Stamfield, it seemed to make a lot of sense at first. Later, we began to have our doubts, but he did make us lose some time at the beginning.'

'I thought you suspected *me*,' said Alec.

'You were one of our suspects, and you didn't have an alibi,' the Inspector pointed out. 'There'll be an inquiry into the investigation, of course, but I'm confident it will show no incompetence on our part.'

'Sure,' said Alec, getting into the back of the police car that had brought him. 'It's lucky for you that Tess and

Ian will be alive to hear the outcome.'

*   *   *

Tess and Ian were kept in hospital overnight and then discharged. Tess's wound had been dressed and was expected to heal well while Ian's ankle was only badly sprained. He was told that within three weeks he should be back on his feet again.

After Marie's funeral, which was covered by reporters from national newspapers and local television, the three friends met up at Ian's house where he was lying on his bed resting his ankle.

Alec and Tess arrived together, both of them subdued by the service but relieved that at last Marie had been able to have a proper funeral.

'So, how does the ankle feel?' asked Alec, once the three of them were alone.

'A bit sore but not too bad. It's definitely on the mend. I won't have to delay my trip round Europe, and that's the only thing that really matters to me now.'

'Is it?' asked Tess in surprise.

Ian took a deep breath and tried to explain. 'The thing is, Tess, having come so close to dying I just want to make sure I live my life to the full. You don't realize how precious living is until you face death.'

'And when you come back?' asked Alec. 'What then? You can't go on travelling for ever. One day you'll have to start living normally again.'

'Sure, I know that, but then I'll go to university and after that there's a career to think about. There are loads of things to look forward to, and I'm not going to tie myself down with relationships and all that stuff. I want to get away, be free and put all this behind me.'

Tess could understand what he was saying, and in a way she was grateful that Ian felt the way he did. It meant that her feelings for Alec wouldn't upset him. For Ian, everything in Stamfield, including Tess, was now a part of his life that he wanted to forget.

'You'll write, won't you?' she asked

lightly.

Ian nodded. 'Sure. At least once a month!'

Tess smiled, but she didn't believe him, and she didn't think he really believed himself.

'What about you, Tess?' he asked. 'What will you do?'

'The same as I intended to do before. I'll go to college, do the childcare course and then work with small children. I like Stamfield. All my friends are here, and all my memories of Marie. I'm not like you—I don't want to forget. I want to remember.'

Ian shrugged and looked away from his friends, out of the window and off into the distance. In his mind he was already in France, meeting up with other backpackers taking a year out before beginning the rest of their lives, and Stamfield wouldn't mean a thing to any of them. That was the way he wanted it to be. He just wanted to get away.

Alec stood up. 'Come on, Tess, we'd better go. Poor old Ian's in pain and we're tiring him.'

Tess frowned. 'Does your ankle hurt that much, Ian?' He hesitated, and then she felt the touch of Alec's hand on her shoulder and realized that Ian really wanted them both to leave. 'I expect it does,' she agreed quickly. 'My mum says sprained ankles are worse than fractured bones, the way they keep aching.'

'Guess she's right,' said Ian with a slow smile. 'See you both again though before I go, right?'

'Sure,' said Alec easily.

Tess bent down and kissed Ian on the cheek. 'Take care,' she said softly. 'And good luck in Europe. Try not to break the hearts of too many girls on your travels!'

Once outside in the street she looked up at Alec. 'Why did we leave so early?'

'Because that's what Ian wanted. In his mind he's already left here. Let's go round to my place. Both my parents are out, so we won't be interrupted.'

In his front room Tess sat on the sofa while he made them mugs of coffee, rummaging around in the cupboards until he found a packet of chocolate biscuits. 'Here you are. Not dieting, are you? I hate girls who won't eat.'

Tess grinned. 'No, I don't diet. I like my food too much.'

'Good. Anyway, I like you just the way you are.'

Tess knew that he meant it, and that this was his way of telling her that he wanted her to be his girl, if it was what she wanted too. It was. She wanted him more than she'd ever wanted anyone and she snuggled up against him with a contented sigh.

Much later, when it was dark outside and time for her to go home, she stirred reluctantly and forced her mind back to less pleasant things. 'Do you think I really knew Marie?' she asked uneasily.

Alec looked carefully at her. 'What do *you* think?'

'I've thought about it a lot,' admitted Tess. 'The trouble is, it isn't the kind of thing I can talk about at home. I mean, Mum and Dad are still in such a state of shock over it all that I have to watch every word I say.'

'You can tell me,' Alec assured her, putting his arms round her again.

'Well, at first, hearing all those things Keith said about Marie did make me feel that I never knew her at all,' admitted Tess. 'But the more I've thought about it since, the more I've decided I was wrong. After all, the good things about her—the way she used to make us all laugh and the fact that she always looked so gorgeous and wanted to make something of her life—they're still true, aren't they? And even if she didn't tell me everything, that was probably to stop us from quarrelling. She'd have known I wouldn't have agreed with her lifestyle and then all we'd have done was argue. The way she lived her life in two separate ways—one in the day and the other at night away from her home and college friends—meant that she kept us all happy all of the time.

'That's the way I'm going to remember her. As someone who was beautiful, outgoing and fun, but who made one terrible mistake.'

Alec nodded. 'Yeah, and we all make mistakes; it's just lucky that most of us don't end up being murdered as a result.'

'You know, the real trouble with Marie was that she got bored so easily,' said Tess, as Alec helped her on with her light summer jacket. 'If she hadn't spent so much time searching for excitement she'd still be with us.'

'Will I be exciting enough for you?' asked Alec gravely.

Tess smiled up at him. 'Yes,' she said confidently. 'I'm not like Marie, I know a good thing when I see it.'

'Even if the "good thing" has a hang-up about car engines and motorbikes?' he teased.

'Yes, even then!' laughed Tess, and together they walked slowly back to her home.

Tess knew she would never forget Marie, but she also knew that now it was time for her own life to move on, and just as Ian had chosen Europe she had chosen Alec and her future career.

Later that night she looked out of her bedroom window and stared down the road, just as once she'd stared waiting helplessly for Marie to return. Only this time she wasn't waiting to say hello, she was saying goodbye.

'Wish me luck, Marie!' she whispered, and for a moment she could have sworn that she saw her sister standing at the corner of the street looking back at her, a mischievous smile on her lovely face. Then, as she blinked, the image was gone, but for the first time since the terrible afternoon at the motel, Tess slept peacefully that night.